SOME LIKE THEM YOUNG
like Betsy, whose idea of a friendly greeting to a stranger was a long and loving roll in the hay with her girl friend waiting for seconds

SOME LIKE THEM BLACK AND BEAUTIFUL
like Melanie, who was always faithful in her fashion to her lover, but wasted no time in filling the gap he left when he was dead

SOME LIKE THEM HAPPY
like Joyce, a hooker who knew every trick of her trade, and loved to share her carnal knowledge

Hardy liked them all—until he found that too much of a good thing could be murder. . . .

Books by Martin Meyers

Patrick Hardy Mysteries

Kiss and Kill
Spy and Die
Red is for Murder
Hung up to Die
Reunion for Death

Dutchman Historical Mysteries
by Annette Meyers and Martin Meyers,
Writing as Maan Meyers

The Kingsbridge Plot
The High Constable
The House on Mulberry Street
The Lucifer Contract
The Organ Grinder
The Dutchman
The Dutchman's Dilemma

HARDY

REUNION FOR DEATH

Martin Meyers

SPEAKING VOLUMES, LLC
NAPLES, FLORIDA
2017

HARDY
REUNION FOR DEATH

ISBN 978-1-62815-365-1

Chapter One

When Patrick Hardy was sure the thief was
making his move, the six foot detective jumped
on his bike and started peddling. His bad left
knee had been strengthened enough by exercise
and therapy so it gave him no trouble as he
chased after his quarry, but being forty pounds
overweight did. As a matter of fact, the extra
pounds were enough to make Hardy almost lose
his prey as he followed him around the corner
into the traffic on Broadway.

Hardy had been hired by one of the local
supermarkets after their delivery boy's cargo had
been repeatedly stolen. The manager of the
store theorized that the kid was doing the stealing
himself and hired Hardy to get the proof. The

police had been informed of the thefts, but their workload was so heavy that the manager was afraid it would take them weeks to catch the thief.

That's why Hardy was out on this mild, sunny, balmy fall day peddling around on a bike trailing a delivery boy on his route instead of watching a movie on t.v., or reading or being in bed with or without a woman.

It wasn't the kid. An hour after Hardy started, he spotted the culprit. The man was dressed in a white jacket similar to the delivery boy's, and rode a bike with a cart in front of it that could have been the twin of the one the boy from the supermarket rode.

The crook's m.o. was simple. When the boy went in with a delivery, the highjacker snipped the chain that immobilized the full cart and replaced it with the empty one, and rode off in full view with his cart of loot.

Hardy witnessed the action and took after the thief. His pursuit was so noisy that the suspect turned around, saw him and peddled away. That's why, instead of merely slowing wheeling up and apprehending the grocery highjacker, Hardy was chasing him through traffic along Broadway.

After both of them were nearly clobbered by a giant trailer truck, Hardy nabbed the thief and turned him over to the store manager who appeared disappointed that his theory about his employee had been wrong. The manager phoned the police and gave Hardy a check.

Hardy took the bike back to the rental place on Amsterdam Avenue and tiredly walked back to his ground floor apartment at 7 Riverside Drive.

His black standard poodle, Sherlock Holmes, was scratching at the door as Hardy undid all the locks that protected his apartment. Inside the dog barked a hello that seemed to imply displeasure at not being allowed to go along for the fun.

"Shut up, Holmes," said Hardy, glancing at the pitifully small figure written on the check. He poured himself a Cutty Sark on the rocks and seated his weary body in the barber chair in his office.

As he sipped his drink, he consoled himself with the fact that Ruby was coming over that night for dinner and bed.

Ruby Red was a stripper Hardy had met while working on a previous case. The case had been a little more exciting than the one he had just completed. He and Ruby had been good friends ever since. Just thinking of the beautiful redhead's full round body made him horny.

He got up from the chair and went into the john to relieve himself and wash up.

He should have ignored the scale, but he didn't. He hoped that the morning's efforts had melted away some weight. It hadn't. Still 220 pounds.

Hardy went into the gym next to his bedroom and made a superficial try at working out, but this depressed him and he returned to the bathroom for a librium. He stared at his good-looking face in the mirror and tried to pretend that his old friend, the double chin, wasn't back. He scowled at his image and went into the kitchen to have lunch and prepare dinner.

With the help of the tranquilizer and his chores and thoughts of the night's activities to come, Hardy spent a fairly happy day.

By he time Ruby showed up that evening the wine and the mussels on the half shell, and the roast beef stuffed with goose liver pate and mushrooms, and the buttered peas and potatos, and the orange Bavarian cream, and the coffee and the chocolate liqueur and Partick Hardy were all in their proper places waiting for her.

So was the freshly sheeted bed with the covers turned down.

And so was Sherlock Holmes.

"Hello, Holmes. That's a good dog. Look at what I brought for you." And she tossed the poodle a new rawhide toy for him to gnaw on. The happy animal raced into the living room with it and purred like a cat as he chewed away.

"Where's my present?" Hardy inquired.

"Hi stud," and she kissed him. "You get yours

8

later, that's just a sample. Hm . . . everything smells so good."

He held her close and nuzzled her neck, savoring her fragrance. He loved the way the light played tricks with her red hair. "Hm. So do you."

Languidly she broke their embrace. "Never mind lover. First you have to feed me. The first time we ever met I told you that, and it still goes. What are we having?"

"Never mind. No kissing and touching, then no staying in the kitchen."

"Yes sir," she said, saluting and kissing him and leaving as ordered.

After dinner they had their coffee and then moved to the couch where they drank brandy and snuggled together and watched television.

Holmes was hard put as to whether he wanted to play with his new toy or join them on the couch and steal tastes of brandy.

During the course of the evening the dog did a little of both. Hardy, who usually didn't mind the animal's antics, grew annoyed. "Holmes, go to bed."

With an air of "I didn't do anything" Holmes obeyed, but his tail was up.

At ten, Ruby switched the t.v. off. "Come on lover," she said.

Hardy grinned. "That's what I like, an honest horny woman. You can't wait until you have my body."

9

She kissed him. "That too, but I also have to get out of here early tomorrow and go home and pack and catch a flight to St. Louis. Brandie got sick so I'm booked to open at a place there tomorrow night."

They were walking towards the bedroom dropping clothes as they went.

Hardy gasped. He always did each time he saw her firm round breasts. He knew it was a corny thought, but each time with Ruby was the first time. "How long you going to be gone?"

"Depends. I'll let you know."

"Do you want me to drive you to the airport?"

"No, I'll take a cab, it'll be easier. God damn it, stop talking so much!"

They were rolling on the bed, their bodies connecting at every conceivable point, and as they pushed and pulled and twisted and turned, he saw each part of her luscious body even though his eyes were closed.

He was at the penultimate moment. He sometimes wished he could stay at this stage and never come down. That point just before orgasm. He opened his eyes and looked at her face. The half smile told him that they were in perfect tandem. The red hair, its fragrance, her fragrance, her breasts caressing his chest, his hands gripping her ass, they were together. He plunged his tongue into her mouth and as he tasted her and the brandy, both their bodies began to buck as they crested and made it together.

In that lush semi-sleep he remembered her doing her SWAN LAKE strip. She had worked with a prop swan and towards the end of the act she rubbed its beak over her breasts and loins. As he visioned this, he reached out to touch those same parts that were lying next to him now. Ruby reached back.

This time they didn't doze off. Afterwards, he got up and fetched them brandy and cigarettes while she changed the sweaty sheets.

When they finished the drinks and ciagrettes, they decided to shower before they went back to bed. While she was toweling him down, Ruby said, "Pat . . . I don't mean to bug you, but you're getting too heavy, just look at yourself."

Hardy didn't answer.

"And you're not a jolly fat man either, you've been very irritable lately. The way you snapped at Holmes this evening, for example. You never did that before. I bet your pressure is up. Why don't you call Dr. Doyle tomorrow and see what she has to say."

He put a finger on each nipple and kissed her on the nose, "You're acting like a wife, but you also happen to be very right. First thing tomorrow, I promise."

By one o'clock the next day he still hadn't called Dr. Merle Doyle. Instead he had eaten a big breakfast and made a lunch from the remnants of last night's dinner and had washed a

11

tranquilizer down with wine and was watching a movie on t.v.

Hardy lay there on the brown and black chaise in his office nodding appreciatively as Bob Eberly sang "Tangerine," while Jimmy Dorsey led the orchestra and William Holden tried to get Dorothy Lamour to kiss him in "The Fleet's In."

Suddenly he snapped off the set and went to his desk and dialed Merle Doyle's office and made an appointment for the next morning. That job completed, he swallowed another librium and took a nap on the chaise.

When the phone rang he made his groggy way back to the desk.

"All right, Holmes, I hear it. I hear it."

Remembering to switch on the newly installed tape recorder, Hardy picked up the phone and said, "Hello."

"Hello yourself, old buddy. Dollars to donuts says you can't guess who this is."

Hardy licked his dry lips and opened his eyes wider. He didn't recognize the voice, but the expression made him think back to college. It would figure that George Lassiter would still be using that expression.

"Hello George, nice to hear your voice after all these years."

"Why you son of a bitch. You old son of a bitch. You did remember. Yes sir, it's me. I'm down here in L.A. from Oregon and I figured I'd look up some old friends, well I couldn't find a lot of them here, so I decided to call a few. That's why I'm calling you in New York. How's the weather there?"

Hardy looked at the phone in bewilderment. He had always thought Lassiter was a bit of a fool, but this was too much. "Very mild for this time of year," he answered.

"It's nice here too. You know, I took over dad's feed and grain operation at home and been making a nice thing of it, even if I do say so myself."

Lassiter went on telling about various money making schemes he had been in on and ended up by asking, "How about you Pat? How've you been making out?"

"I'm doing well, George."

"That's good. What have you been doing?"

Hardy used to enjoy announcing his profession, but as the years went on, it tended to embarrass him. "I'm a private detective."

"Well if that don't take the cake. Pat Hardy, a detective. Well then, you're just the person I should ask. Do you remember Ben Alsop? Of course you do, you and he were good buddies. I'm trying to locate old Ben, and since he lives in New York and you're a private detective, maybe you could locate him for me and let me know where he's at. I'm not going home for another week, so I'll give you my address here in L.A. and the one at·home too, and you send me a bill on this, you hear? After all, what are

13

old friends for, if not to throw business each other's way?"

George Lassiter gave him the two addresses and reiterated about being sent the bill. After he hung up, Hardy replayed the tape to check on the machine's efficiency and thought back.

Strange, he had been reminded about George and Ben and the rest of the guys at the end of last summer, just before he started working on the Lane Peterson case. He'd received the Summer Alumni Bulletin, and it had sent his memory back to when he was at school.

Hardy laughed out loud at the fact of his being concerned about weighing 220 pounds when back in college he'd weighed 320. But that was well before the man in the barbershop had put a bullet in his stomach. In a strange way the man had done him a favor. He'd recovered from the gunshot wound and lost enough weight for the army to draft him and slim him down some more. 180 pounds, to be exact. And though Hardy was an ingrained and self-admitted coward, the army also trained him, or rather programmed him, to become a very deadly fighting machine when the occasion arose. This skill and the lack of any other had led Hardy into his present occupation.

But he was mixing his memories up. Back at school he was still the 320 pound fat boy while Lassiter had been a handsome second string quarterback who got to play quite a few games and score both on and off the field.

Then there had been Lassiter's two friends, Al Ricci, the smooth operator, also on the football team, who knew how to do the mambo and all those other dances, and Marvin Leon, another jock, the hustler who worked his way through college by waiting on tables.

And Ben. A guy Hardy could sympathize with. Patrick Hardy was fat and unwanted and Benjamin Alsop was skinny and pimply and unwanted. Hardy's outlet had always been food and books. Ben doted on crossword puzzles and photography. The two misfits became friends in their misery.

Hardy had never thought about it before this moment, but it was really strange how Lassiter and Ricci and Leon, who had been an exclusive troika unto themselves, had done a turnabout and brought Ben Alsop into their fold . . . and Ben being Ben, had gotten them to admit Hardy to their company.

A strange quintette.

Something else tickled his memory. It wasn't the kind of thing that interested him then, but he found the memory interesting now. There was that girl who disappeared. What the hell was her name?

Hardy got up to turn off the tape recorder and reset it and then shifted his mind into how he would go about locating Ben Alsop. Too bad they had never kept in touch. If he found him, it would be nice to see him again.

15

Chapter Two

Hardy took out his college yearbook and looked at all the young faces to remind himself who was who. Then, after a brief search, he found an old address book with Ben's phone number in it. No answer.

Remembering that Ben's folks had lived in Riverdale, he got the number from information, but after he dialed it, an operator came on the line.

"Sorry, your call did not go through, may I have the number you're calling?"

Hardy told her.

"I'm sorry, it is temporarily disconnected at the customer's request."

"Operator, can you tell from your records how long that's been temp . . ."

"No, I'm sorry, I have no other information, sir."

"Okay, thank you, m'am."

Hardy leafed through the old address book again. Al Ricci was listed. On a chance, Hardy tried it.

"Hello."

This was followed by a confusing outburst in a language he couldn't even place. Obviously Al Ricci's old number now belonged to someone else. Hardy apologized and hung up. He checked with information, who gave him three Albert Ricci's in Manhattan, one Al Ricci and one A. Ricci. He discounted the A. Ricci as probably being female since many women had themselves listed by initial only to avoid obscene phone calls.

The Al Ricci listed was not the one he wanted.

One of the Albert Riccis was located in the East 50's. Hardy tried that one first.

"Hello."

"Al Ricci?"

"Yes."

"Al Ricci, this is Pat Hardy."

"Oh, from school?" Al Ricci said. "Hi Pat."

"Hi, how are you?"

"Okay."

This was getting more and more asinine by the moment, and Hardy could feel the wariness in the other man's voice. He could appreciate it; he had felt the same thing when Lassiter had called him. Remembering to flick on the neglected tape recorder switch, he decided to come right to the point.

"I'll tell you why I called, George Lassiter called me, and after discussing his business, and how much money he was making, and how he lost a few bucks on race horses he bought and now sold . . ."

"Same old George," Ricci interjected.

"Well anyway, he asked me if I knew where to find Ben Alsop."

"Oh . . ."

Hardy noticed the remark but kept talking. "And I wondered if you knew."

"Let me think now . . ."

"I have an old number . . ." said Hardy.

Ricci continued, "I happened to see Ben about a year ago."

"Uhuh," Hardy mumbled.

"I'm not friendly with him at all. I saw him about a year ago . . . is Lassiter in town?"

"No, he's in California for a little while. He told me since he had a little free time on his hands, he was trying to touch base with a few people . . . he'll probably be calling you himself."

"Okay," said Ricci, "let's see if I have anything on Ben."

"I had a number for him downtown . . ."

19

"Hold on."

There was a silence while Ricci checked. He came back on the line. "No, I don't have anything on him."

"Yeah, well I had this number on St. Mark's Place . . ."

Ricci cut him off again, "I know when I met him he told me that he lived in Mexico or something, part of the year. Other than that, I don't know what to tell you."

"I tried his folks' number in Riverdale, but the operator told me that the number was temporarily disconnected."

"I don't know," said Ricci, who sounded as if he was tired of the whole conversation, "When I met Ben he told me his folks still lived out there . . . maybe something happened to them."

"No," said Hardy, "I don't think so. It was disconnected at their request."

"Oh . . . well . . ."

Hardy persisted. "How've you been doing?"

"Fine . . . fine. I'm a big disappointmnt to my father. I didn't follow in his footsteps down on Wall Street . . . believe it or not, I'm an interior decorator. Doing very well too, a lot better than some of my friends who are working on the Street. How about you?"

"I'm a private detective."

"Is that a fact?"

After that, there was another silence which

Hardy broke when he had a sudden thought. "What about, what's his name, the guy with the two first names, Marv Leon?"

"Tell you the truth," said Ricci, "I just don't know what ever happened to him. No, I haven't seen him or Ben in a long time . . . is Lassiter coming here?"

"He didn't mention it," said Hardy.

More silence until Hardy decided to end Ricci's obvious discomfort.

When he hung up he replayed the conversation but this time he wasn't checking the equipment. The entire situation was beginning to take on a very jarring note.

Lassiter, Ricci and Leon were very tight back in school. Why hadn't Lassiter called Ricci instead of him? Also, he understood why Ricci wasn't too interested in Ben, but why the turn-off on Marv Leon? It all really didn't seem to fall together.

Annoyed at being drawn into the situation, Hardy dialed Ben's old number again. This time someone picked up and said hello.

"Ben?"

Hardy reminded himself about the recording equipment and turned it on again.

"Is this. . . ?"

The flaky voice on the other end of the line stopped him. "Is there someone else who lives where you live?"

21

"I beg your pardon? . . . I'm trying to locate . . ."

"It sounded like someone else picked up the phone, that's why I asked," said the man.

Hardy mentally cursed at the noisy switch on his equipment and resolved to have it replaced.

"Oh . . . it's probably the F.B.I.," he tried to joke. "I'm trying to locate Ben Alsop. Is this Ben's number?"

"Yeah, but he's in California"

This was the topper. "He's in California? . . . Would you have his address or phone number?"

"No," said the sleepy voice.

"You have nothing on him?"

"He's going to Hermosillo."

"Huh?"

"In Sonora . . . Mexico."

"You mean to his house?" Hardy guessed.

"Yeah, right."

"There's no way I can reach him there?"

"Hermosillo. Write him in Hermosillo. He's either leaving today or tomorrow."

Hardy managed to get the address out of him before he hung up.

Hardy knew that the most efficient thing to do was phone Lassiter with his information, but he really didn't want to talk to him again. He called Western Union instead and wired Lassiter giving Ben's address in Mexico, and telling him that ironically enough, they were both in California at the same time and maybe he could locate him at that end himself.

Good. Over and done with. He flipped through T.V. Guide to see what he could watch while he prepared dinner.

Chapter Three

Hardy awoke the next day with the information nagging at his brain, something about how Ben Alsop and Marv Leon had hooked up and gone into some sort of business together.

The thought annoyed him. He had nothing to do with it any more. He had done what Lassiter had asked, and now it was over. Besides, he was hungry and it was Thrusday, Laura's cleaning day and he was in no mood to listen to her advice, or to the various soap opera characters she watched.

His aim was to get up, eat and get out and get over to see Dr. Merle Doyle. His appointment wasn't until noon, but he had to get out of the house.

Holmes, always in a good mood, was dancing around in a morning greeting. Hardy nearly stumbled over the poodle on his way to the john.

He could feel his own tension as he yelled at the animal. "Damn it Holmes, get out of the way."

Ruby was right. He had never before taken his frustrations out on the dog. He was definitely in a bad way. He hoped Merle Doyle would be able to offer some sort of solution.

He used a glass of pineapple juice to wash down another librium. The capsule didn't seem to help. He burned his hand on the frying pan as he cooked up a batch of wheat cakes and left the bacon on too long.

Hardy smothered everything in maple syrup and wolfed it down, drinking three cups of coffee and smoking two cigarettes in the process. Then he quit the apartment as soon as possible, ignoring Holmes' protesting barks, not caring that he had skipped the dog's morning trip to Riverside Park.

Outside he walked down to the Boat Basin and lit another cigarette. The water stank so much he gave it up as a bad idea and meandered downtown toward his doctor's office, chain smoking as he went.

Merle Doyle waved hello to him as she saw to another patient. He sat there thumbing agitatedly through an old Esquire. He was early for his appointment.

26

The doctor must have realized the state he was in because as soon as she was finished with her patient, she had the girl send him into one of the treatment rooms even though it was an hour before she was due to see him.

Hardy tensed up as she wrapped the material around his arm. He closed his eyes when she started pressing on the bulb so he wouldn't see the reading on the blood pressure gauge, but he could sense the starting and stopping of the throb in his arm and he knew without her telling him that the reading was high. He swallowed as she silently unwrapped the paraphernalia from his left arm and tried again on his right. High again.

"My friend," she said quietly, "you are in bad shape."

"Tell me something I don't know."

"Get on the scale."

When she saw his weight, she shook her head at him. "Get dressed and come into the office."

She was already there when he entered the wood paneled room. Usually Hardy's natural curiosity made him read one of the many diplomas or certificates on the wall or glance over the titles of the medical books on the shelves. This time he merely slumped into the chair in front of her desk and waited.

Dr. Doyle turned down the radio cutting off the flow of Chopin and looked directly at him. "Two major priorities: get the pressure down, get the weight down. If you're not careful one

27

of these days you're going to have a stroke. How would you like to spend the rest of your days as a vegetable in a hospital bed?"

She wrote two prescription blanks and handed one to him. "Get this filled as soon as you leave here. Take two in the morning and two at night. I want you back here in one week so I can take a pressure reading. I thought we could handle it with tranquilizers, but apparently we can't."

She handed him the second blank. "This is the name and address of a weight reducing place. You used to be able to discipline yourself, but . . . go see them, they're reliable people. If you do what they say and follow the rules, you should be back down to 180 or 185 pounds in a fairly short time . . . how's your knee?"

"Okay, I guess."

"Good," she said crisply. "I mean it Pat, 185 pounds!"

Usually Hardy had some sort of lecherous remark to make to his attractive doctor, but this time he didn't have any "cute" things to spout. Instead, he smiled wanly at her pretty face and said nothing. Then he took the two slips of paper and nodded at her and left the office.

He was hungry. He was so hungry his stomach ached. Banishing all common sense, he stopped for a French vanilla ice cream cone and ate it as he walked up to Hank Bianco's drugstore.

He was just finishing it off when he said hello to the druggist.

"You know, Pat, I sell ice cream too," Hank Bianco said as he took the prescription blank and went behind the partition to fill it.

"Yeah, but no cones." Hardy stepped aside so a customer could get to the counter to be served by one of the other druggists.

"All right," said Bianco, raising his voice slightly, "Buy other people's ice cream, but don't come here and flaunt it at me."

Hardy wiped his mouth with his handkerchief. "Just put the pills from the big bottle into a little bottle and stop pretending what you do is so mysterious. It's not like the old days when you had to make it up with a mortar and a pestle."

"Quiet," Bianco said as he emerged, "You want the whole world to know? Charge or cash?"

"Charge," said Hardy.

"Why do I even bother to ask?"

Hardy shoved the vial of white pills in his pocket. He started to leave and then stopped. "I can never remember Hank, which one is the mortar and which one is the pestle?"

Bianco gestured dismissively and turned to a new customer. Hardy forced a laugh at his forced joke and tried to pretend a merriment that he didn't feel. His session with Merle Doyle had made a bad day seem even worse.

Holmes started barking as he opened the door. He patted the poodle and said hello to Laura.

"Hello Mr. Hardy." The phone rang but the

service answered and her attention was back to her soap opera.

He went into his office with Holmes tagging behind, and called his service only to find that it had been a wrong number.

He went to the bathroom and washed down two of the blood pressure pills. He was hungry, but Laura's presence made him too nervous to eat. He went to the hall and took Holmes' leash from the wall rack. He was about to whistle for the poodle, but he didn't have to. Holmes was already there, tail wagging wildly.

"I'll be in the park, Laura."

"Yes, Mr. Hardy."

While Holmes cavorted in the open field, Hardy sat on a bench and tried to relax. He thought of the other piece of paper Merle Doyle had given him and wondered what he had done with it.

A short search located it in his shirt pocket. He read it and laughed and then read it out loud, "Fat Limited", and laughed again.

He liked the name. Besides being a good name for a weight reducing outfit, it was similar to the name he had chosen for his own investigating firm, "Trouble Limited," which he more often than not forgot to use when he answered his phone . . . he would call "Fat Limited" on Monday, no sense in ruining a perfectly good weekend.

Despite all his plans for a sumptuous food

gorging weekend, it was destroyed before it ever began. Friday morning he called Merle Doyle and told her about his new problem.

"I've been in the john all morning with one of the worst cases of diarrhea I've ever had."

"Take some kaopectate and forget about it. Sometimes those pills do that. Use the kaopectate for a few days and then stop, by that time your system should be used to the pills."

"Are you sure of that?"

"No."

Saturday and Sunday were just as bad, if not worse. To add to it all, it rained. By Monday his system was under control and he thought about putting off his call to "Fat Limited" for a few days so he could enjoy the meals he had planned for the weekend and had been forced to miss. He would have done just that except for the pair of pants that didn't seem to fit the way they used to.

All of his clothes had gotten too tight lately, but he hadn't paid attention to the situation in the hopes that it would go away. It hadn't. He readied several pairs of pants to take to the tailor and dialed "Fat Limited."

"Certainly, Mr. Hardy. Always room for one more. We'd be delighted to have you. The class meets tonight at eight."

Hardy sneered at the jovial voice and hung up the phone. He left the apartment and walked over to Broadway where he dropped off the pants with the tailor, bought a few pair of cheap cords, and picked up the newspaper and that month's issue of Penthouse.

Back at the apartment he went to the gym and worked out, annoyed at how difficult situps had become. After a shower he treated himself to cold shrimp and sour cream with curry while he read the newspaper and the magazine.

That night, wearing his new cords and feeling much lighter because the pants didn't bind, he went to his first session at "Fat Limited."

It wasn't as depressing as he'd expected. So many of the other people were much heavier than he was, and it didn't take too much rationalization on his part to convince himself that he was only slightly overweight.

He filled out forms, paid money and was directed around a corner.

This was depressing. The mat on the floor leading to the room where they were all to meet concealed a scale. What was worse, the results were flashed over the entrance way in red lights.

221 the light flashed at him as he went in.

He listened to the lecture. When the lecture was over, he filed out with the rest and received his list of food he could eat and was informed that his ultimate goal was 180 pounds.

That night he skipped his usual snack while he watched television. His stomach hurt so much from being empty that he had to take a tranquilizer to get to sleep. In the morning he worked out in the gym, and after a short trip to Broadway, he returned with his altered pants and groceries that included skimmed milk and cottage cheese. After what he considered a very scant breakfast, he changed his clothes and took Holmes for his morning romp.

They were on their way back when Hardy saw her coming from the opposite direction. She seemed to be looking for an address. She was one of the most stunning women he had ever seen. He hoped the address she was looking for was his. When she stopped in front of his entrance way, he almost choked Holmes in his eagerness to get there before she left.

"Excuse me," he said, trying not to shout, "If you're looking for Patrick Hardy, that's me."

She turned and said, "I am looking for you. My name is Melanie Ryan."

"Why don't we go inside? Holmes, sit!" Hardy could barely manipulate the key, he was so hung up on looking at Melanie Ryan. Now he knew what black and beautiful really meant.

The front door was open. "Watch the first step," he warned, and then eyed her as she walked down the hall. What he saw was just as good from the back as it had been from the front.

While he worked on unlocking the inside door, and Holmes was dancing around at the prospect of company, Hardy said, "What seems to be the problem?"

"I'm not sure."

33

He tried to digest her words as he led her inside. No matter, he would ask again. They had all the time in the world. He offered her a drink, but she shook her head. He considered one for himself but remembering the caloric content of a shot of whiskey, decided to pass.

"Sit down, please," he said, "Holmes, go to bed!"

The poodle gave a muffled bark and marched out.

"You didn't have to do that," she said, "I like dogs."

Hardy appraised her all over again as she sat in the chair in front of his desk. She was more of a caramel color than black and her hair was soft and wavy and natural looking. Except for lipstick she wore no make up and her skin seemed baby smooth, and he wanted to touch it. He hadn't noticed it before, but her nose was slightly crooked. Now that the face was fully inventoried, he was ready to check out her figure again and see if her breasts were as full and firm looking as they had appeared at first glance.

All this was taking place during a fraction of a second, but he got no further.

"Ben Alsop told me to get in touch with you, here read this," and she handed him an envelope. "The trouble is, some postman or somebody got it wet. Most of it has been washed out."

Hardy took the faded letter out of the envelope and saw what she meant.

"Dear Mel,
I'm in Cali   go to Hermosill
few days. If everything goes as expected I should be calling   Monday and then you can come and   here.

Problems, got a call yesterday fro   some-body called   checking me out. And today I had the funniest   that   one was followi me from L.A. to Sa   iego.

Two names to rememb ,   at Hardy. If you don't hear f m me by Monda
  b Pat . Of all the people I've ever known he's probably the only one except you I can trust. I   seen him in years but   you've played the games I have   you to dig deep to ind a friend. Tell Pat
    the one and   in
it   The proof is
        my apartment.   if you don't hear from me by Monday, get in touch with P
        ove you
        Ben"

Even the letters and words he could read were barely discernable. Hardy put the letter on his desk and got up to get himself a drink.

"Is anything wrong?" Melanie Ryan asked.

That was a good question. Just as he got up, he felt very dizzy. But it passed. He decided against the drink and sat down.

"No, nothing's wrong, at least not with me.

From what I can make of this, there seems to be something wrong with Ben. Did you try calling him when he didn't call you?"

"No. There's no phone at the house in Mexico."

"Let me take this to a laboratory, maybe they can bring back what's been washed out. In the meantime, tomorrow I'll check out the apartment."

Melanie Ryan breathed a big sigh and closed her eyes. Now that she had unloaded to him, she seemed to be in a deep funk.

"Are you all right?" he asked.

"I think I'd like to lie down."

He led her to the chaise. With concern that was overshadowed by lechery, he helped her to lie down and went so far as to take her shoes off.

"That's better, isn't it?"

Her mouth attempted a smile and nearly made it. "Yes."

"How about that drink now?"

"I'd really love it, scotch and water . . ."

Hardy fixed her drink and then poured himself a short one. "Are you hungry?"

"Famished, I've been so upset since this came and then when Ben didn't call last night . . ." She let that sentence dribble off and started a new one. "I guess I've been too confused to even think of eating."

"Well you're thinking of it now . . . that's a good sign."

Hardy went into the kitchen and took out several wedges of cheese and set them on a board along with some water biscuits.

"Why didn't you telephone?" he called out to Melanie Ryan.

"I don't like phones. Too simple for people to lie over the phone. I like face to face contact."

Hardy was listening, but he was also looking fondly at the cheese. In a surge of discipline, he took a carrot out of the refrigerator crisper and haphazardly scraped it clean.

"Do I pass the test?" he called as he scraped.

"I think so. Besides, if Ben trusts you, I trust you."

Hardy came back into the office to find that Holmes had joined her on the chaise. Melanie was scratching the dog behind the ear and really smiling now. Hardy laughed as he set the food down and shoved Holmes over so he could sit.

"That's a contradiction."

She cut a bit of cheese, ate it, cut some more and asked, "What do you mean?"

He watched the food going into her mouth, micro fantasizing about each and munched his carrot. "You had to see me in person in order to know if you could trust me, but you trusted me before you ever met me because Ben trusts me."

She pondered this for a second or so, and while she did Hardy watched and wondered what she would be like in bed. If things went along well, maybe he would find out. True, she seemed to be Ben's girl, but what was a girl between friends.

Melanie sipped her drink, "You're right . . . it is a contradiction, but it isn't . . . more like a double check. Could I have another drink?"

Hardy jumped up. "Sure thing." While he poured he talked just to keep the conversation going. "How'd you find me?"

"You're not the only one who can be smart. Thank you," she said, taking the drink. "It wasn't hard to figure from the letter that 'at Hardy' and 'Pat' and 'P' all added up to Pat Hardy. Then I looked you up . . . I let my fingers do the walking. You happen to be the only Patrick Hardy in the Manhattan telephone book. What's the "A." stand for?"

"Anthony."

"Tony, I like that better than Pat. If I wasn't so hung up on Ben, I could really go for you, Tony."

Hardy made his move. Her lips were soft and giving, and her tongue seemed to have a life all of its own and her body seemed so right in his arms.

Suddenly she stopped. Hardy pulled back to see what was wrong. Melanie was smiling but she was shaking her head.

"I admit there's a physical attraction, but I'm a one man woman, and right now that one man is Ben Alsop. You're nice Tony, but ... whoops. I think I'd better call you Pat the way everyone else does. Tony makes too many images in my mind. I thought Ben said he trusted you?"

"Just about certain things," Hardy answered.

Melanie nodded, understanding. "I see." She laughed. "Ben's exactly the same way ... the bastard. But I love him and I want you to find out what's wrong. Will you do that for me?"

His mind was going in twenty different directions. It was a favor for an old friend; Melanie had turned him on; the only job he had had in weeks was that stupid grocery job; why the hell hadn't he sent Lassiter a bill; and there was no way he could discuss a fee on this case.

"Did Ben ever talk to you about me before?"

"No," she said, putting on her shoes.

"Then he doesn't know that I'm a private detective."

She stopped, one shoe off and one shoe on. "No ... and neither did I until just now. That makes it perfect. Then you know what to do ... and you will help? Please."

"Sure. Now that you know me, is the telephone okay?"

"Sure," she smiled. She went over to his desk and wrote on the memo pad. "Here's my address and number. Let me know as soon as you can."

"Right. I'll call you in a couple of days, or you can call me if you have a mind to."

"Thank you."

He took her to the door and ambled back into his office. As he thought about how nice she felt to touch, Hardy absentmindedly ate a piece of cheese. He gave one to Holmes and was about to gobble up another when he realized what he was doing. He started to get up and take the food back to the kitchen, but one frustration was all he could handle that day.

"Screw it," he said out loud and poured himself a large scotch and used it to wash down the rest of the cheese.

Chapter Four

Hardy smoked a cigarette and reread the letter Melanie had given him. He put a sheet of paper in his typewriter and put down what he thought it told him:

1. Ben was in California.

2. On his way to Hermosillo.

3. Supposed to call Melanie Monday (Never did)

4. He received a call from someone about another someone checking him out.

There were two thoughts buzzing about in Hardy's head. The first one was fairly obvious, and he typed it.

4A. That could be a reference to my call to

the flakey character I talked to. The one who gave me the Hermosillo address.

5. Someone might have been following Ben.

The second thought was still buzzing. When it came to rest, it didn't make much sense to Hardy, but he put it down anyway.

5A COULD LASSITER BE INVOLVED IN ANY WAY???

Hardy looked at 5A and nearly x'd it out. Instead he lit a new cigarette and kept reading and typing.

6. The proof of whatever Ben meant to tell Melanie was someplace in his apartment.

That was all he could glean. Maybe this list would turn out to be only an exercise if the lab could bring out what had been washed away. Hardy took the sheet of paper from his typewriter and pinned it to the cork wall next to his desk.

He was hungry. The cigarette tasted lousy. He squashed it out in the ashtray and put Ben's letter in his jacket pocket.

The newspaper he read on the subway downtown had nothing of interest in it and only served to kill time till he got to his destination.

After dropping the letter off to be analyzed, he walked to a different subway and took the train to Second Avenue. From there he walked to St. Mark's Place.

He remembered this area when he was a kid. His father, who loved Jewish cooking, had hustled him and his mother down here often. He was glad his father wasn't around to see the changes that time and people had made.

The proliferation of winos and junkies and motorcycle types made Hardy very nervous. When he had located the number he was looking for on St. Mark's Place, he wasn't too sure he wanted to chance going up to the apartment. Ben's name wasn't on any of the letterboxes, most of which were gaping wide open, but there had been a notation in Hardy's address book.

He mounted the three flights with some vigilance, expecting he-didn't-know-what to come leaping out at him.

Hardy could hear what sounded like Indian music coming from the other side of the door. There was an old fashioned bell, at eye level, in the center of the door . . . he turned it. The music made it hard for him to know whether his turning had produced any sound, but it must have because a female voice called through the door, "It's open, come on in."

The decor was bare brick and tie-dyed burlap, but he didn't take much notice. Standing in the middle of the room was a tall semi-nude female of about twenty-five. Her brown hair was in a long braid. The one breast he could see was quite lovely. The other was covered by her pale green painting smock. He liked the legs too, even though her feet were dirty. The girl was viewing herself in a full length mirror and trying to recreate the image on the canvas in front of her. It wasn't bad . . . neither was she.

"Excuse me . . ." Hardy started to say.

"Hi," said the girl, "you looking for Jack?"

"No, I'm looking for Ben."

"Oh . . . he's in Mexico. Jack should be back in a couple of hours." She had a slight Southern accent.

Hardy attempted small talk. "That's very good."

"Yeah, it is. There's wine in the ice-box, I mean if you want any."

He went to the old fashioned refrigerator that stood in the corner of the room. There didn't seem to be anyone else in the apartment.

He poured himself a cup of white wine. "Do you want any?"

"No thanks," and she dabbed more paint on the canvas, "not my thing at all. Strictly grass. No morning afters, if you know what I mean. You holding?"

"No, I'm sorry."

"Me neither. It's a drag. I hope Jack remembers to get me some. He's so hung up on his own bag sometimes he forgets about me."

Hardy sipped the cold wine. "Isn't this Ben Alsop's apartment?"

The girl considered his question and then stepped back to look at her painting. The smock opened wider. Hardy appreciated the view but repeated the question.

"Well," she said, "It's mine and Jack's and Trudy's and Phil's and Harry's and Nancy's and June's and Vi's and Ben's." She nodded her head several times. "Yeah, this is Ben's apartment. Alsop? Is that his last name? I didn't know that. Are you sure you're not holding?"

He shook his head.

"I know," she said, "let me paint you. Take off your clothes."

Hardy, who had been in a semi-erect state ever since he had entered the apartment, simultaneously pulled in his stomach and started to strip.

"Shit," she said startling him. "I don't have any canvases left . . . you want to ball?"

The frankness of her question so amazed him that the hardness in his pants shriveled away. This was followed by flashing pictures of v.d. posters.

She had removed her jacket and was arranging several pillows on the floor. The sight of that lovely ass banished all the v.d. posters from his mind and brought back his excitement.

Still in his shorts and tee shirt, he moved to join her on the pillows.

"Hey, what are you, some sort of clothes freak? Take 'em off. Take 'em all off. I dig looking at bodies. That's better. Not bad. If you lost a few pounds, you'd really be beautiful."

He was too excited to be put off by her remark about his weight. As they kissed and he ran his hands over her body, she said, "By the way, my name's Betsy, what's yours?"

He started to say his name, but by that time she was biting his tongue. Now she was licking his ear. "Bite me. Pain's a groovy turn on."

As she said this her nails were raking his back. They had started in the missionary position but had rolled over. Betsy was gyrating and bouncing and bouncing and moving in a series of panic filled movements that Hardy had never experienced before. He took his eyes from her body and looked at her face. Her mouth was in a strained tight line as she strove to make it. Hardy had been about to explode but the look became a challenge to him. It appeared that Betsy had rarely, if ever, made it and his ego being what it was, Hardy didn't want it to be that way with him.

As he accelerated and varied his movements, a portion of his mind went back to another woman: The Duchess. She had just finished serving him Grand Marnier in milk and was telling him how marvelous he was in bed. "Darling, you are the best. Even better than a young Russian I once had, K.G.B. But he went through training . . . doing multiplication tables in his head and such. All technical. But you are a natural lover . . . I hope you weren't doing multiplication tables while you were making love to me."

He hadn't then, but he was doing them now.

Betsy started to make painful little moans. Tiny cries of frustration. He changed his tactics and pretended he was going to withdraw. She pressed closer. He pulled away. The ritual continued until her tiny little cries dissolved in one gigantic scream.

Knowing she was there, Hardy concentrated on his own pleasures and let himself go. Release . . but when it happened, it was a disappointment. He was sure he had made it, but it didn't feel as complete as it usually did. He attributed it to the multiplication tables and vowed never to use the method again. What was the use of putting it off if when it happened it didn't feel like anything?

He turned his attention to Betsy who was asleep and smiling blissfully.

As he stood up, he felt dizzy. What the hell was the matter with him? He got dressed and went to the door. Betsy called to him from the pillows, her Southern accent more pronounced now, "You come back, you hear."

Slowly he went down the stairs. He was really dizzy, and his body was a collection of tiny hurts. Besides what Betsy had done with her nails and teeth, the damn pillows had been burlap, too.

Outside he found a candy store. He changed his mind about the chocolate bar and had an egg cream instead. Then, on a hunch, and to save himself another trip downtown, he called the lab where he had left the letter.

"Nothing so far Mr. Hardy. We ran some

tests, but they all came up negative. He must have used a soft pen."

"Which means?"

"No indentations that we can find. We'll go for greater magnification. If that doesn't work, maybe we can come up with something that can reactivate the ink. So far everything we used hasn't worked. That letter really got soaked, and it wasn't dried properly. Try us tomorrow. We should know by then."

He went home and prepared dinner. It was a strain, but he left the lemon butter sauce out when he made the shrimp. That and the plain salad and the dietetic grapefruit slices made up his entire meal. He had left out the one slice of bread he was entitled to to make up for the egg cream, but when he was through eating, it was as though he had not even begun. He cut a very thick slice of bread and smeared it with butter. To compensate for this, he drank his coffee black and sugarless.

Hardy rose to put the dishes in the dishwasher. He was dizzy again. Maybe it was from hunger?

Boring t.v. programs were topped off in a pleasant way in the form of "The Barkleys of Broadway." He watched Astaire and Rogers and Oscar Levant and remembered the first time he had seen the film. So while Fred Astaire was singing "They Can't Take That Away From Me," all Hardy could think of was popcorn and hotdogs and cokes.

48

In the morning he slept late. But when he got out of bed, he nearly fell down. This dizziness was getting ridiculous. No workout. No shave. Coffee and toast, and he went to see Merle Doyle.

When the attractive doctor came into the treatment room she said, "I'm not taking your pressure the mood you're in. Lie down and think calm thoughts. I'll be back in about ten minutes."

Hardy didn't say a word and did as he was told.

His thoughts first concerned themselves with the ceiling. He closed his eyes and thought of Merle coming back in the nude. That was nice but not calculated to calm him down . . . unless of course he could make it with her . . . the next scene had him thrashing about the burlap pillows with Betsy. No. That was part of his anxiety, the fact that his orgasm had been so unsatisfying. Now he was imagining Melanie in the nude. Maybe . . . but that was a might be. . . . Ruby, that was an accomplished fact. He dwelled on remembered sweet after moments with Ruby.

"Good, you're smiling. You look a lot calmer. Let's see what we have."

Merle Doyle checked his left arm. Hardy looked at her questioningly. She said nothing and moved to check his pressure on the right side.

"Well, what is it?"

"Quiet," she said, listening to the beats and watching the gauge. Hardy closed his eyes.

"Patrick, I'm proud of you. 120 over 85. You don't look any thinner, but I'm very pleased with your pressure. We'll skip the weigh-in this time. Come into the office."

Hardy didn't recognize the piano music on the radio. He sat down and listened.

"Carl Maria von Weber," she said to his unasked question. "I didn't know anyone had ever recorded it . . . not bad. And that goes for you too. Not bad . . . tell me, what's the trouble?"

He then proceded to describe the dizzy spells and the peculiar type of orgasm he had experienced.

"Relax Pat. The solution is at hand. They're both side effects of the pills you've been taking. The less than full orgasm you described is what is known in the trade as 'shooting blanks'. At least it didn't make you impotent. That's been known to happen, too."

Hardy burlesqued a groan.

Merle Doyle chuckled. "Don't worry about it," she said, "I'm so pleased with the results, I'm cutting you down to two pills a day . . . from what you tell me, your love life isn't being impaired . . ."

He sat up straight in the chair. "Not being impaired? What the hell do you call this? So far these pills have given me the runs, made me dizzy, and made me shoot blanks. And now you tell me that they might make me impotent. I wish that just once I could get a medicine that does what it's supposed to and that's it . . . no side effects."

"Pat . . . with the reduced dosage these symptoms will almost disappear. For a while get up slowly, **especially in the morning** when you **wake up.** In a few weeks it will probably stop. So will the shooting blanks . . . you ought to be grateful. Some men start shooting blanks without ever taking this medicine."

"When does it start?" he asked.

"Any time after eighteen. So you're ahead of the entire male world . . . I'm sorry I mentioned the impotency to you . . . knowing how suggestion prone you are, it might happen."

She stopped for a pause and said, "Then again, knowing you, that's one thing that would never happen. I'll see you in two weeks. Congratulations."

The only thing on Hardy's mind as he left the doctor's office was making it with someone. It didn't matter who. He just had to find out how his performance was. He hadn't taken that day's dosage yet. It would wait until after he had been to bed with someone. Ruby was out of town.

Melanie. He was extremely attracted to her and that would make the experiment even more interesting. He almost ran back home. Holmes, sensing his excitement, barked louder and longer when Hardy came in.

Hardy found Melanie's number on the memo pad and dialed it. No answer.

Betsy. As far as he knew the easiest lay in town was sweet Betsy. As the cab took him downtown, he hoped that she would be alone again. He had the driver drop him on Tenth Street and Second Avenue and he walked the rest of the way.

The gaunt figure inching down the stairs scared Hardy so much he felt as if his heart had stopped. The bearded man looked straight through Hardy and kept inching. Hardy took a breath and continued on up.

No Indian music this time. He twisted the bell to the front apartment.

"In."

He opened the door. Betsy and another girl were sitting on the floor smoking. The room was redolent with pot.

"Hi," said Betsy, "If you're looking for Jack, he just left."

So that was Jack. Hardy wondered if he was the person he had spoken to over the phone. He considered going after him. The consideration didn't stay long in Hardy's head. Jack was in no state to talk to anyone, and Hardy had other problems to solve.

Betsy was offering him her cigarette. "Join the party. We have enough stashed for the whole world."

He was tempted, but he wanted to keep his head straight; otherwise he wouldn't be sure if the experiment worked. He was figuring out ways to get rid of the other girl when Betsy said, "I forgot, wine and balling is your thing," and she was slipping out of her Superman tee shirt. "You know where the wine is . . . do you mind if Vi watches? Vi digs watching. Vi, this is . . ."

"Pat," he supplied, and the blonde girl who was dressed in a sari waved at him and giggled.

This was going to be some test.

Hardy went through the motions of pouring the wine, but he set the cup down and went back to Betsy and her friend and the pillows. He made a face as he remembered the pillows and thought, what the hell, and stripped off his clothes.

At first he was self-conscious, but Betsy was all over him and he forgot about Vi. Remembering what Merle Doyle had told him made Hardy the frantic one this time.

His self-destructive imagination supplied the thought: he wasn't going to make it. He thrust himself harder and deeper. The fear of incompletion was frightening.

Wait! It was there. Building! He couldn't rush it. It was there! And something new was there. Vi was there contributing to his happiness.

Then in one big rush all the joys obliterated all the fears and the floodgates opened and Hardy was free. He drifted off into a short contented sleep.

A hand was rubbing his belly. He could still

smell the pot. Even though he hadn't smoked, he was sure he had a contact high.

"Come on, Pat," said sweet Betsy. "Now you and Vi, so I can watch."

Later, as he whistled "Sweet Betsy From Pike", a very tired and very much assured and happy Patrick Hardy left Ben Alsop's apartment on St. Mark's Place.

Chapter Five

After he left Betsy and Vi, he grabbed another cab and visited the laboratory where they were working on Ben's letter.

"Sorry, Mr. Hardy. Excuse the pun, but it's a washout."

He thanked the man, wrote out a check, and took another cab home and went to bed.

When he awoke, he imagined a dinner of onion soup with a lot of cheese and fried frogs legs served in tomato sauce and zabaglione for dessert. He had to settle for beef liver, spinach and an apple.

He had finished off the apple, eating it right to the core, and was just pouring his coffee when the phone rang.

"I hear it Holmes." He switched on the tape. "Hello . . . 'Trouble Limited', Patrick Hardy speaking."

"Hello, Pat, it's me, Melanie."

"Hi Melanie. Sorry I didn't call, but I didn't have anything to report. The lab couldn't do anything with the letter and I've been to St. Mark's Place twice. The apartment's a dead end."

"St. Mark's Place!" she exclaimed. "Damn it! I forgot all about that dump. Ben hasn't lived there for years. It's still under his name, but he just keeps it as a crash pad for friends. The truth is Pat, Ben can't seem to forget he's getting older. The old apartment is part of his beatnick days. He spends part of his time being an over-aged hippie or flower child, or whatever the name is now, and the other part being a successful business man . . . I was so distracted when I left you and I've been so busy running the store that it never occurred to me that you meant the old apartment and didn't have the keys to the new one. If you want, I could take you there tomorrow morning."

"That would be fine. What store?"

"The health food store that Ben and I own. It's really his, but he gave me forty-nine percent of the place when he bought his partner Marvin out."

"Would that be Marvin Leon?"

"That's right," she said, "Do you know him?"

"Yeah. He and Ben and I went to college together."

"Well, he and Ben have been together since school, I guess, and they were in a lot of businesses together. Ben likes that. Get a business, build it up and sell it for a profit. He gets bored easily. Anyway, a few months ago he and Marv decided to split up and Ben bought him out. There were some other business deals besides the store, but I don't know much about them. I've got to run. I'll be by in a cab about ten-thirty tomorrow morning, is that all right?"

"Fine," and he hung up the phone and switched off the tape. He got up from his desk too fast and there was a slight touch of dizziness, but it went away almost as fast as it came. While he was standing, he followed an impulse and wrote a new entry on the list on the cork wall.

"7. Marvin Leon ????"

After that he massaged his aching stomach and walked back and forth in front of his bookcase looking for something to read. God, he was hungry.

He climbed the small ladder and found "Looking Backward" by Edward Bellamy hidden behind another book. He took it and a box of melba toast to the barber chair and read and munched until the eleven o'clock news was due to go on.

He decided not to watch the news and kept reading. At eleven-thirty he had his choice of a talk show, a horror movie or Tyrone Power in

"Jesse James." It was no contest. He turned on the set in the bedroom and watched Jesse and his brother Frank fight the railroad and tried to pretend he wasn't hungry.

He fell asleep before John Carradine fired the fatal shot into Jesse's back. Consequently he was rudely awakened when the tv station came back on the air in the morning.

After a quick workout and a shower and shave, he breakfasted on grapefruit, one egg, one slice of toast and black coffee.

He felt slimmer. He didn't want to get on the scale in case he was wrong . . . but he felt slimmer. He put on one of the suits with the altered pants and combed his hair three times. By that time Laura was there. He greeted her brightly.

"How've you been, Laura?"

"It could be worse, Mr. Hardy, it could be worse. Thank the Lord, I'm better off than most people."

"That's nice," he answered, not really listening. "I'm going to take Holmes out for his walk and then I'll be gone for the rest of the day. If the phone rings, let the service pick up."

Since it was close to ten-thirty Holmes had a very short trip to the park. He knew it and he let Hardy know he knew it.

"All right Holmes, that's enough. I'll make it up to you tomorrow." He repeated his phone instructions to Laura and went outside just as Melanie pulled up in a cab.

He got in and she told the driver the address. Their bodies were barely touching as they sat next to each other on the ride across town, but her proximity was more than enough to turn him on.

When the cab dropped them at the Madison Avenue address, Hardy was impressed. Melanie had told him that Ben was successful, but if this large, modern structure with its massive lobby and many uniformed employees was any indication, he was very successful.

The entire apartment was done completely in black and white. Hardy whistled his appreciation, then he asked, "Did he have a decorator do it?"

"No, he did it all himself. Ben is a man of many talents. Why do you ask?"

"No reason. Just waiting for the name of Al Ricci to come up, then the trio would be complete."

"Huh?"

"Nothing," he answered, "Just a random thought."

She laughed, "But don't you get it? He did it this way for me. He said since our life was a contrast in black and white, he would make his apartment the same way."

"Very sweet," said Hardy, examining one of the many cameras lying about the apartment. "A burglar could clean up on cameras alone in this place . . . what's wrong?"

"Things don't look right," she answered. "I don't mean to be melodramatic or anything, and I can't exactly tell you why I'm saying this, but I have the funniest feeling that somebody's been in this apartment and searched it and then put things back in place."

"That's interesting," said Hardy and he opened the door and looked at the lock. "There are scratches on the lock, but that could have come from someone picking it or from normal use. Why don't you have a good look around and see if anything is missing or if you can find something out of the ordinary . . . you know, what Ben seemed to be referring to in his letter."

"All right," she said, taking off the jacket of her gold pants suit. Hardy admired the thrust of her breasts against her brown checked shirt.

Deprived of all this when she went into the bedroom, he sat on the long white couch and picked up the crossword puzzle from the black marble table. Ben had worked them in pen, but Hardy used the pencil that was lying next to the book. As he searched for a fresh puzzle to work on, he noticed that Ben had left a few unfinished. Very well, he would test his mettle against his old friend. Every few pages he found a word and filled it in. This done, he started a new puzzle of his own and was halfway through it when Melanie announced that she was done.

He shoved the book in his pocket and asked, "Do you still feel the way you did? Has somebody been searching the place?"

She nodded. "Definitely. They were very neat, but so's Ben, and certain things aren't the way they should be . . . and I couldn't find anything . . . hell, I didn't even know what I was looking for. What happens now?"

"Now you pour yourself a drink and relax and I'll search."

Hardy checked book bindings and floor boards and walls. He even unscrewed the plates on the wall switches and outlets and looked in the little recesses behind them. Nothing.

By the time he was through, it was mid-afternoon and his stomach was demanding attention. He had planned on making a pass when he was through searching, but much to his own surprise he was too hungry even for that.

There was an Italian restaurant in the neighborhood and Hardy was in no mood to pay attention to his diet . . . besides, he had missed lunch.

"Come on Melanie, I know of a great place to eat near here."

"Good idea," she agreed, "I'm starved."

On the way to the restaurant he bought a paper and shoved it in his pocket.

"You shouldn't do that. It's no good for your suit. Look at you, a magazine in one pocket and a paper in the other."

He took both offenders out of his pockets and held them in his hand. "Do you mother and boss Ben around like that too?"

She smiled wistfully. "Every chance I get."

In the restaurant, after he had ordered the antipasto, she excused herself to go to the lady's room. "I don't know what's wrong with me. I should have gone in the apartment."

During her absence Hardy looked through the paper. A short item caught his attention:

"Firemen discovered a hoard of marijuana while combating a fire on the Lower East Side this morning. According to an official source, more than fifty pounds was found in an empty apartment."

There was more to the story, but the most interesting part of it was that the address given was Ben Alsop's apartment on St. Mark's Place and that the police had no idea as to the identity of the tenant. Hardy made a mental bet with himself that it was the crash pad.

He turned the page and saw another short piece. This one was datelined Sonora, Mexico:

"The body of a murdered American who was a part time resident here was found in the capital city of Hermosillo last night. The body of Benjamin Alsop was found just outside his home. He had been shot twice in the head. Police are searching for a motive in the mysterious murder. The dead man had over three hundred dollars in American money in his pockets and all of his credit cards. His wrist watch, and an emerald ring were still on his person. Local authorities admitted they were without a single clue or witness."

He reread it.

"Don't you know it's bad manners to read . . ."

Melanie stopped speaking when Hardy looked up from the paper. She reached over and took it from him. Her eyes scanned the page, and then she saw it. She read it once, turned the paper back to the front page, folded it neatly, and returned it to Hardy.

"Pat, please get me out of here while I can still control myself."

He rose, peeled a few bills from his money clip and dropped them on the table. Then, holding Melanie by the elbow, he guided her out to the street. "Where to?" he asked.

"My apartment . . . Sutton Place."

Hardy started to search out a cab. Melanie grabbed at him. "Never mind . . . take me back to Ben's."

The walk there was without incident. It wasn't until they had gotten out of the elevator and he was unlocking the door, that she started sobbing.

He closed the door and led her to the white couch.

"Ben, Ben. Ben." Over and over she keened his name.

Hardy was uncomfortable. He sat down next

63

to her and patting her on the shoulder, muttered some cliche or other.

She turned and clung to him, desperate for comfort and solace . . . he held her in his arms savoring the feel of her form next to his with only fractional thoughts of Ben's death or her needs. He held her closer feeling her breasts through all the layers of clothing that separated them.

Melanie kept crying and growing more and more frantic in her grief, while Hardy grew more and more excited by the fact of her. He moved his head to kiss her . . .

The turning of a key in the lock was unmistakable. Hardy redirected his mental processes and placed a quieting hand over Melanie's delicious mouth, shoving her lower on the couch. The door opened and two men came in. The man wielding the key was very familiar.

Hardy popped his head up and quipped, "Detective Friday, I presume?"

The stocky black cop let go of the keys and made a move to his holster. Halfway there he stopped and used the hand instead to rub his mustache. "For Godsake, what the hell are you doing here?"

"I'd like to ask you the same question," said Hardy, eyeing the well dressed Hispanic man behind Friday.

Friday and his companion came into the apartment. The companion closed the door. Hardy lit a cigarette and gave it to Melanie, who was still trying to control her tears.

Friday spoke. "Excuse me miss, I'm Detective Gerald Friday. This is my I.D. and this is a search warrant," he said, showing the named items. The cop went on, "This gentleman is Lieutenant Luis Mendoza from Mexico."

Mendoza nodded politely when he was introduced, then quickly glanced around the large living room. He was waiting for Friday to continue. When he saw that the New York cop was deferring to him, Mendoza said, "I am investigating the death of Mr. Benjamin Alsop. Mr. Alsop was shot to death last night in Hermosillo." The Mexican had almost no trace of an accent. "This is Mr. Alsop's apartment?" he asked more out of politeness than a need to know.

Hardy lit a new cigarette for himself while Mendoza was talking. "Gentlemen, this is Miss Melanie Ryan. She was Ben Alsop's fiancee and he was an old friend of mine. Up until I read about his death in today's newspaper, I was investigating what I thought was his disappearance."

"Mr. Hardy is a private investigator," Friday said to Mendoza.

Mendoza took in the information and said, "I would like to proceed."

Friday cleared his throat and said to Melanie, "I realize how rough it must be on you, and I'd like to be able to leave and come back another

65

time, but we're going to have to search the apartment now."

Melanie's tears evaporated. She jerked her head up. "Don't patronize me. You do what you have to do. Pat, will you take me home, please."

In the cab Melanie muttered under her breath.

"What?" said Hardy.

"Who the hell does your friend think he is?"

"What do you mean?"

"Get off it, Pat, you're not dumb." She managed a small laugh as she said, "You're white but you're not dumb . . . I've gotten that attitude before from black men when they see I've been paired off with a white guy."

"No," he protested, "Gerry's not that sort of a guy."

"All right," she answered, searching her bag for a cigarette, "Call me paranoic. God, what a day."

Hardy gave her a cigarette and lit it. She took one drag and let it dangle from her hand as they rode the rest of the way in silence.

When they arrived she said, "Pat, don't come up. I've got to be by myself . . . are you going to stay on the case? . . . Please."

What else could he say? "Of course I am. I'll call you as soon as I know something. You call me if you need anything . . . okay?"

"Okay."

He had the cab take him home.

During the trip he thought about what Melanie Ryan had said about Gerald Friday. It was almost the same accusation Friday had leveled at him when they were both investigating the Kate Arnheim case. He replayed the cop's voice over on his mental tape recorder.

"Maybe the fact that a black man made it with a girl you were screwing galls you more than you would like to say, even to yourself."

He didn't dwell on the fact that Friday and he might be on opposite sides of the same coin except to think that it was probably that they were both sexists rather than racists.

Instead, he remembered Kate: Kate's figure was almost the ultimate of Hardy's fantasies. Long, thin, shapely legs, an almost boyish rear end and large breasts that didn't sag. Slowly the dress rose. Those lovely legs. The black pubic patch. Her belly glistening with sweat. Her lips were red and hungry. She moved her long dark hair away from her face and knelt at the foot of the bed . . .

"Here we are," said the driver.

Hardy came back to reality, paid the driver off and went into his apartment. Laura gave him a telegram that had come just after he left. It was from Ruby, telling him that she had another booking and was going on to Toronto once she closed in St. Louis.

Hardy tossed the telegram on the desk along with the crossword puzzle book and the newspaper, and scratched Holmes' ear while he thought about what he should do or not do. What he finally decided was not because of his dedication to law and order, or his friendship with Detective Gerald Friday, or even the fact that Ben was dead and no longer required his loyalty . . . but just because he figured if the police dug around in certain areas, they might come up with something that Friday would pass on to him and it would help him solve Ben's death and find whatever it was Ben had hidden and get him out of this mess. . . . then maybe he and Melanie . . . Hardy picked up the phone to dial Ben Alsop's number and realized he didn't know it.

He called Melanie. She gave him the number, but was very terse when he asked how she was. He hung up and wondered if it was due to what had happened or were there other reasons. At times like these Hardy never knew whether he was being extremely perceptive or exceedingly neurotic. He shrugged off the conundrum and dialed the number of the Madison Avenue apartment. As he hoped, Friday answered the phone.

"It's me, Pat."

"Hello Pat, I kind of thought there was something else you wanted to tell me."

"That's interesting," said Hardy, "Until this minute I didn't know that . . . but I'll trade you. When you introduced Lieutenant Mendoza you never mentioned whether he was a local cop who worked where Ben was killed or whether he worked for the Federal police, or what."

There was a lot of dead air on the phone while the private detective waited for Friday to answer. When he was sure he would not, Hardy broke the silence. "All right, I guess I owe you. In today's paper there was a story about firemen finding a hoard of pot when they went to answer a call on St. Mark's Place. If the fire originated in the front apartment on the third floor, you might be interested in knowing that Ben Alsop was the tenant of record there."

Hardy pulled the phone away from his ear as Friday whistled into it. "Private Detective, I thank you. That happens to be very interesting. So long."

"Is that it?" Hardy said incredulously.

"Sure," said Friday.

"I mean, you just admitted that what I told you was important. Now how about me? Don't you have anything to tell me?"

Friday paused for a moment and said, "Yeah, there is one thing . . . that Melanie Ryan is sure one hell of a good looking woman . . . see you around, Private Detective."

Chapter Six

It was Friday morning. Hardy had finished his workout and skimpy breakfast and was sitting in the barber chair watching, "Only Angels Have Wings", on television.

Holmes was on his back on the floor in his cute pose, his eyes shining plaintively as he waited for his belly to be scratched. During a commercial Hardy scratched it. When the movie came back on and Hardy went back to his barber chair, the dog got annoyed and kept pushing at Hardy's foot with his head so that Hardy would pay attention to him.

Hardy was trying to watch the picture and think of the case at the same time . . . and not think of food. He knew his only lead was finding

Betsy, or Vi, or Jack. He planned to go about doing that after the movie was over.

As Cary Grant was taking the new plane up for a test flight, the doorbell rang.

Holmes barked and Hardy activated the street t.v. set.

It had been a long time, but Hardy recognized Al Ricci. He hadn't seemed so on the phone, but the man on his screen pursing his lips and impatiently ringing the bell again, seemed a little gay to Hardy. The memory of how girl crazy Ricci had been back in school amused Hardy when he compared it to the Al Ricci he was looking at now. He went out to let him in.

"Hello, I'm looking for Pat Hardy, I understand he . . ."

Hardy pulled Holmes back into the hall. "Come on in, Al. What's the matter? Don't you recognize me?"

"For heaven's sake," said Ricci, "I never would have recognized you. You're so thin, you must have lost a ton."

"A hundred pounds is a little closer to the mark."

As he led his old schoolmate back into the apartment, Hardy mused about his present problem of trying to lose forty pounds because all those who knew him now said he was fat, while Al Ricci, who knew him then, thought of him as thin.

"Did you read about Ben in the papers?" asked Ricci.

"Yes, I did." They were inside. "Here it is. The place I call home."

"Nice," said Ricci, wrinkling his nose, "nice, but a bit eclectic."

Hardy lit a cigarette, "I'm sorry you don't like it . . ."

"I didn't say that," said Ricci.

Hardy continued with his thought, ". . . It's a pity you've never seen Ben's apartment. I think you'd really appreciate it."

"Oh, you've been to Ben's apartment?"

"Just one foot ahead of the police . . . I found it very interesting." In mid-conversation Hardy suddenly realized that he was stringing Ricci along without knowing why . . . but Ricci acted as if he knew what Hardy was talking about even if Hardy didn't.

The interior decorator appeared to tense up. "What do you mean you found it interesting?"

"Nothing. Just a random remark."

"You found something?"

"Such as?" Hardy said, squinting at him through the smoke of his cigarette.

"Well, Ben had something that belongs to me . . ."

"Such as?"

Ricci ignored the repeated query and went on in the same tentative vein. "If the police were to find this something, it might turn out to be . . . well, embarrassing."

Hardy pressed what seemed to be an advantage, "Such as?"

"Pat, now that you're a private detective, I suppose this would be right up your alley." Ricci was sweating. "What would you say if I retained you to recover my property and agreed to pay you ten thousand dollars for it?"

"I would have to say that I don't exactly know what you're talking about."

Ricci's voice went up in pitch about five notes. "And I think you're a liar. All right, fifteen thousand dollars. Give me the package and no questions asked."

"Plenty of questions asked, Al. One in particular. Would you please describe the contents of the package for me? If you identify it properly, maybe we can see about getting it back to its rightful owner."

The voice was still high. "God damn it, don't play games with me!"

Holmes started barking. Hardy calmed the animal down. "Lie down, that's a good boy." Hardy felt warm and slightly dizzy. He was starting to get very annoyed with Al Ricci. Slowly and evenly he said, "I like things nice and calm, Al. When things are not nice and calm, I get upset and my dog gets upset. I don't particularly like that to happen. I also don't like to be called a liar. Now either tell me what you want; and softly . . . or get out."

Ricci wiped his brow with a silk handkerchief. "First, I'm sorry. I take back what I said, but if you can be cagey, so can I." And here he giggled, "I mean, if you know what's in the package, then there's no need for me to tell you . . . if you don't know, then it would be stupid for me to tell you. On the assumption that you know what I'm talking about . . . and even have the package in your possession . . . on receipt of that package I will pay you ten thousand dollars."

Hardy was beginning to enjoy this. "I thought you said fifteen thousand?"

"Then you do have it?"

The detective lit another cigarette from the old one smoldering in the ashtray. "Goodbye, Al, I'll be in touch."

"All right, fifteen thousand, but that's all I have."

Hardy fingered the lapel of Ricci's Cardin suit. "I doubt that. Say goodbye, Al," and he guided him out of the apartment with Holmes barking his agreement all the way.

Hardy wandered all through the apartment. Holmes dogged his heels while he tried to figure Ricci out. Obviously . . . or apparently . . . or maybe, the proof Ben referred to in his letter and the package Al was so anxious to get was one and the same.

He found himself at the refrigerator. He

opened the door. The cottage cheese and skim milk were a disappointing sight. He slammed the door shut and thought about caviar, and avocados, and melon, and ham, and clam chowder, and steamed clams, and breasts of chicken made with cheese, and shepherd's pie, and potatoes, and bread and butter, and roast wild duck made with port wine, and steak, and baked potato with sour cream, and pizza, and tapioca, and chile and hamburgers . . .

Hardy broke off his reverie in front of the cork wall and rubbed his aching stomach. He took the list down and examined it.

After finding a ballpoint pen that worked, he made a few additions. Entry number 8 was: Al Ricci.

Entry number 9 was a triangle with the names Lassiter and Leon, and Ricci at each point, and a question mark in the center.

He crossed the triangle out and changed it to a rectangle. Hardy wrote out the three names again, each in a corner, then he put Ben Alsop's name in the fourth corner. He was about to redo the question mark when instead he added a triangle to the top of the rectangle, making it look like a child's drawing of a house. At the new point he wrote Melanie Ryan's name . . . then he put in the question mark.

He thought about seeing Melanie. One, she was on his list. Two he was sure if he played it right he could ball her. The mere thought of the possibility turned him on.

After reconsideration he realized that, on both counts, it might be a little too soon. Maybe if he had some news to bring her? This led him back to his original plan of the morning: Betsy.

He took Holmes out for his walk and then lunched on non-sweetened canned pears and cottage cheese and dry toast and tea without sugar. Feeling as empty as he had before eating, he set Holmes' ground chuck out to thaw and went outside to go downtown.

First, he went around the corner to the main part of the building to get his mail. Pete, the doorman, regaled him with the story of how one of the women tenants was almost mugged the day before and got away by running into the building where Fred, the night man, actually slammed the door in the muggers' faces.

"Two of them, Mr. Hardy," said Pete. "Two kids, maybe eighteen years old . . . one black and one white. Integration is finally here, huh Mr. Hardy?"

"What did the woman do?"

"She called the cops, but now she says she's going to go out and buy sneakers so she can run faster."

Hardy smiled at the remark and threw away the junk mail he had received. He rejected the thought of the subway and went back to the Drive to wait for the bus. As he turned the corner, he saw one pulling into the stop. Disregarding traffic, he ran across the street before it could pull away.

Winded, he sat down. At least the running hadn't made him dizzy. He was starting to get a little concerned about that.

With no paper or mail to read, he checked in his pocket for the puzzle book. He had forgotten, it was on his desk. He looked around at his fellow passengers. The woman across the aisle stared at him sullenly. Hardy looked away. Towards the rear he noticed a fat-faced type. Since he had started gaining weight, Hardy was always noticing fat-faced types. This one was extra weird. Besides his unkempt mustache and his granny glasses, he wore a jacket with buttons pinned all over it. The largest one bore the picture of an eskimo and the inscription, "Don't eat yellow snow."

Hardy relegated him to the Jukes Family and started reading the ads over the windows when a new female passenger moved to sit in a vacant rear seat between fat-face and a young girl.

The young girl blurted out, "You can sit, but don't touch me."

The woman shied away and sat in a different seat.

At the next stop, a man went to the seat between fat-face and the girl and the incident was repeated.

"You can sit, but don't touch me."

"What are you talking about?" the man bellowed. "I'll do what the hell I want."

The girl cringed as the angry man started to sit.

Fat-face stood up. "For God's sake. Here, sit in my seat. Don't you have any sense? Can't you see she's disturbed?"

"What did he say? What did you say about me?" the neurotic girl demanded of Fat-face.

"I said that you're a nice girl and that you don't like people crowding around you . . . and I don't blame you."

"Okay . . . you can sit down if you want . . . but don't touch me."

Hardy didn't know whether to laugh or be saddened by the situation, but considering Fat-face's actions, it reminded him not to be so quick in judging or misjudging people.

Feeling somehow guilty that it wasn't he that had come to the girl's defense. Hardy got off the bus and began to walk. Nervously, he searched himself for the little pill bottle. He found it and dry swallowed a librium capsule. Although he knew it couldn't take effect that fast, he felt better almost immediately.

He was in front of a bookstore. He went in and killed the better part of an hour browsing. Aware that he was being lazy and a little leery of the area he would have to haunt in order to find Betsy, he made a deal with himself to get into a cab and tell the driver the first thing that came into his mind.

"Yes sir?" said the cab driver.

"Follow that car."

"Huh?" said the driver, not even bothering to turn around.

"Never mind," said Hardy. "Just wanted to see if you were paying attention."

"Huh?"

"Second Avenue and Fourteenth Street," said Hardy, feeling foolish about his first request and wishing he hadn't made his second. What he wanted to do was tell the cabbie he had changed his mind and that he would like to go to Riverside Drive, but by this time he felt too self-conscious to do anything but sit there until they arrived in the East Village.

After over-tipping, he quickly scurried away from the driver's line of vision.

Now what?

Now that he was here, how the hell was he going to find Betsy. She could be somewhere around here or uptown or in Cairo, or in Mexico.

Bars were out. If she was around, it would either be in a coffee house or in a juice bar.

She was in neither.

"Hello, there."

He didn't know whether his luck was being bad or good, but there she was right in front of him.

"I said hello," said Betsy. "Are you holding?

I got burnt out of my place and my stash went up in smoke." She laughed. "You should have seen those people standing around watching the fire and taking a lot of deep breaths. I wasn't in the apartment when it happened or they might have shipped me home in a pine box. It might have been Jack, he's always nodding off with a cigarette in his mouth. I guess it wasn't. The papers say the apartment was empty . . . I haven't seen him around, have you?"

He shook his head.

"You got any money?"

Hardy nodded.

"Great," she said, "I know where we can make a buy. All right? All right," and she took his arm and led him downtown.

All Hardy could think of was whether or not her sandal clad feet were warm enough. He guessed that they were. He guessed that she was too, even though she was only wearing jeans and a Mexican poncho . . . and from the way those clothes outlined her form, he also guessed that the word "only" was very apt.

On Tenth Street he spotted a delicatessen and dragged her in.

"Hey, wait a minute," she protested, "Not here."

"Maybe not for you," he answered, "But it is for me."

He ordered a lean cornbeef on club bread and

french fries and a cream soda. Betsy insisted that all she wanted was a coke.

Hardy told her not to go away, and he went to the rest room in back of the store. Inside he bolted the door and separated his money so that he had ten dollars in one pocket and twenty in another and his money clip with the rest in still another. Since he was there, he used the facilities and went back outside.

For a moment he thought she had skipped on him. Not only was she still there, but she was gobbling up his food. He ordered again and sat down. "I thought you said you weren't hungry."

Betsy smiled through a mouthful of cornbeef. "I was wrong."

She finished quickly and nagged at him to do the same when he lingered over the first real meal he had had in days.

"Take it cool, Betsy. It'll all come together. Take it cool. Isn't that what you kids are always saying?"

"What do you mean, you kids?" she demanded.

Hardy's food-concerned mind quickly calculated that he had made his first tactical error with Betsy.

"Steady kitten, no offense. Just a bunch of words put together, that's all."

"I guess you're right," she admitted, "Come on, let's go."

He swallowed the remains of his soda, enjoying the carbonated drink to its fullest. After a suppressed burp, he lit a cigarette and paid the check out of the ten dollar pocket.

She took him downtown past the number streets and over to Stanton Street. There she left Hardy out on the sidewalk while she went into a hallway. Before he could get jumpy, she came out with a pimply faced teenager. The boy stayed back while Betsy came over to Hardy.

"He says yes. The very best. Fifty dollars."

Hardy looked at her. All he could see in her eyes was urgency. "Too high . . . I mean, what we're getting is a little pot. It's not like we're getting into anything heavy, just a little pot. I'm right, aren't I, Betsy?"

"Yeah, sure, just pot. But it's a seller's market. Things are scarce these days. I'll see if I can get him to come down."

She and the boy parleyed some more. She waved Hardy over to them. The boy was shielding a plastic bag with his coat.

"Give him twenty-five," said Betsy.

Hardy removed five from one pocket and added it to the twenty from the other and held it out to the boy. He didn't let go of it until Betsy had the bag in her hand and then under her poncho.

"Hey Mister."

He turned to look at the boy, but he heard the clatter of sandals even as the boy spoke, "I think your girl friend's running away with your stuff."

The private detective watched that marvelous ass running away from him and didn't even think of running after it as he realized she had pulled one of the oldest con games in the world on him.

He turned back to see if the boy knew anything about Jack, but the boy was gone too.

Even though he had the good grace to smile at himself for being such a fool, it still bugged him.

"Shit" he said, "And double shit" as he walked back to Second Avenue and the subway entrance.

Chapter Seven

Because he was tempted to steal the dog's ground meat, Hardy fed Holmes early. Then he went to the phone. He dialed Manhattan North and hit the switch on the tape recorder. The operator put him through to Gerald Friday.

"Yes Pat what is it?"

"Thought you might like to know a little about the people who used to stay in that apartment on St. Mark's Place."

"Give."

He told Friday the three names and described Betsy and Vi and Jack.

"Thanks Pat, we here, hard working members of the City Police Department, appreciate it when you romantic private detectives condescend to come down from your ivory towers of beds and beautiful women and give us working stiffs a needed helping hand."

"Shove it. Do you have anything I can use?"

"Sorry, Pat, the lid is on," said Friday, and hung up without even saying goodbye.

Hardy placed the phone back in its cradle and turned off the tape recorder. It occurred to him that turning the tape on and off each time he used the phone could become very tiresome. He decided to make it all automatic. He went to get his tools and as he worked on the hookup, Hardy realized that his telling Friday about Betsy was a petty way to vent his anger on the girl but he rationalized that he should have told the police about her and her friends in the first place.

Job done, he was about to test it when the phone rang. He kept the bottom drawer open so he could check the tape. He picked up the phone . . . the tape was rolling. Success.

"Trouble Limited, Patrick Hardy speak . . ."

"Pat, it's me, Melanie. Somebody's been through my apartment, but they weren't neat about it the way they were at Ben's."

He could hear her voice going strident, "It's a mess. Pat, could you please come over . . . now."

"Be right there."

He hung up but delayed leaving until he had played back the tape. Satisfied with his work, he grabbed an apple from the kitchen and went out as Holmes barked his displeasure at being left alone again.

When Hardy got to the Sutton Place apartment, he saw that Melanie wasn't exaggerating. What had once been a sectional sofa was now in a lot more pieces than its designer had intended. There were bits of blue material and stuffing from the sofa all over the beige rug and the wicker chairs. The bedroom had fared no better. Melanie, who was alternately puffing at her cigarette and running her hands through her hair, was fit to be tied. Over the phone she had sounded like she was ready to cry. Now she looked like she was looking for someone to punch in the nose.

Hardy looked around and said, "What a dump."

"What?" A lot of Melanie's anger came out in that one word.

He took a step backward. "Steady, I'm not the one who did this. Just trying to make a joke."

She picked at one of the wicker chairs trying to rid it of all the bits and pieces that were clinging. "I don't get it."

"I was imitating Elizabeth Taylor, imitating Bette Davis in . . . never mind, it was a very bad joke . . . I have an idea."

She gave up on the chair "Yes?"

"You have someone who cleans the apartment?"

"Yes," said Melanie, "My mother shuffles in

twice a week . . . I'm sorry Pat, that wasn't called for. I use an agency . . . wait a minute, are you saying they might have done this?"

Hardy laughed "No . . . I wasn't being a detective. I was just trying to be helpful. Why don't you call them up and have them send three or four people over right now while I take you out to dinner. When we get back, the place will seem almost normal and it won't seem so hard to take. In answer to your question, no I don't think your cleaning service had anything to do with this. With you out at work, they could have done it . . . but if they had, they would have been a lot less obvious . . . no this was done by someone who was desperate and in a hurry. . . maybe someone who knows you. Does anyone else have the keys?"

"The only one is . . . was Ben."

"Did you see them at his apartment?"

"No."

He picked up the phone and handed it to her. "Then if he left it in his apartment, maybe that's where our inquisitive friend found it . . . call the cleaning people and tell them it's a quadruple emergency."

While she dialed, Hardy thought about another possibility. If Ben Alsop had been carrying the keys while he was in Mexico, maybe his murderer had them and maybe it was he who had paid this little visit to Melanie's apartment. When she hung up he said, "I think you'd better call a locksmith too and have him change the locks."

She looked at him for a brief second, nodded and called information.

The cleaners arrived in less than half an hour, the locksmith wouldn't be there until the next day.

He took her to a nearby Hungarian restaurant. The food wasn't on Hardy's diet, but by this time he really wasn't paying much attention to it.

Melanie was as hungry as he was. After the apple soup, she ordered pork goulash while he had meatballs made with paprika and sour cream. On her second beer and his third scotch he said, "If I sound nosey, I'm sorry, but it's the only way I know how to find out things . . . I noticed a few of your things at Ben's and a few of his at yours, I mean, I figured that's what I . . ."

"You figured right . . . go on, ask your question?"

"Why the two apartments?"

"Ben wanted it that way . . . he was right, too. Both of us are . . . we're very sensitive people, and sometimes we liked being alone . . . it sure avoided a lot of problems. He had his life, I had my life, and we had our life . . ." Suddenly Melanie realized the unfortunate choice of words, and she finished the macabre pun, "and now he doesn't have his life."

Hardy braced himself for the new flood of tears. They never came. Instead, Melanie switched to scotch and the two of them drank until the restaurant closed.

The cleaning men were gone when they got back to her apartment.

"That's a little better," she said when they got inside, "Pour me a drink while I get comfortable."

He smiled at the cliche and waited impatiently for her to reappear. When she didn't, he went into the bedroom.

Melanie's nude body made a startling contrast against the lime green rug and scarlet red dressing gown she clutched in her hands. She was beautiful. The trouble was she was also out cold from too much booze.

For a long time he just stared. First at her dark caramel nipples that showed in a sort of bas-relief against the lighter tone of her firm breasts. Then at the St. Christopher's medal that hung between them. It amused him that the thought of the Saint's non-identity was even in his mind.

His eyes went to her mouth, opened in heavy breathing, and back to her breasts and the rest of her lovely body. Hardy sighed and lifted her from the floor to the bed shivering in frustrated pleasure as he touched her.

On the chance that it might awaken her and also because he had to, Hardy kissed the luscious mouth. Melanie moaned and smiled in her sleep and rolled over and hugged the pillow.

He was at a loss as what to do. He knew the smartest thing was to go home, but he kept hoping she'd wake up. He went to the bathroom. The brown leather shower curtains and the scents of her bath powders and perfumes turned him on even more than he had been. He wet his face with cold water and went back to the bedroom.

Melanie was still asleep . . . and still nude . . . and . . .

He wandered about the room looking at the furniture and opening closets and drawers and picking up things and putting them down. Anything but leave. All the while he was engaged in these dumb activities, he kept glancing over to the bed, to enjoy looking and to see if she had opened her eyes.

It was during his third examination of the Sheraton secretary that he decided he was being silly. The carved eagle perched on top of the piece of furniture seemed to agree. Hardy winked at the bird and started to go. Melanie said something in her sleep. He rushed to the bed, but she was still out of it. Then, knowing he was behaving like an adolescent, he lay down on the bed next to her, hoping perhaps if he waited long enough she would wake up.

He kissed her again. "Melanie?"

No response.

Hardy lay back and closed his eyes.

An hour later, after dozing off several times, he finally decided to leave. When he got home, he ate five slices of white bread and butter and washed them down with a glass of skimmed milk sweetened with a lot of chocolate. Then he took a cold shower and went to bed.

He couldn't sleep. There was nothing on t.v. and none of the books in the bedroom appealed to him. He got out of bed waking Holmes, but not stirring him, and went into his office. None of the books there seemed interesting either. In sheer desperation he pulled out "The Charterhouse of Parma."

As he passed his desk, he noticed the crossword puzzle book and took that, too. In bed he started the Stendhal book, but couldn't get past the first paragraph. He remembered reading it in school and had always planned to read it again. Not this night. He put it aside and picked up the puzzle book.

Soon he was fast asleep and dreaming.

Melanie was lying on a large bed, but the bedspread was designed to look like a crossword puzzle, so were the walls. She was naked, but in his dream, she was awake. She was calling to him. Hardy ran towards her. He couldn't seem to get any closer. Why was it so hard to run? He was heavy. The way he was back at school. 320 pounds of blubber. Fat Pat Hardy.

Melanie was calling to him. "Pat, I want you. I need you."

He was on the bed. He was on Melanie . . . but he couldn't do anything. He was impotent . . . and Ben was taking pictures of him being impotent and all the other guys were razzing him. He could see George Lassiter and Marv Leon and Al Ricci . . . they were all laughing at him.

Suddenly Melanie was very still . . . She was dead. Hardy yelled at Ben to stop, "Give me those pictures. I don't want my mother to see them."

He awoke just long enough to realize he had been dreaming and then he went back to sleep. In the morning when he awoke, he remembered the dream. He didn't know what it meant but the thought of ever being 320 pounds again made him resolve to get back on his diet and stay on it.

He was thinking about lunch when Melanie called to tell him that the locksmith had installed new locks and to apologize for passing out on him. She didn't pursue the subject any further and neither did he. Then she said something about having to go to the store and hung up.

Over the rest of the weekend Hardy kept to himself and his diet.

Monday morning he jumped out of bed ready for the world and nearly fell down. He was so dizzy he had to sit on the edge of the bed for over fifteen minutes before it cleared up.

Despite the dizzy spell, he went into the gym. His workout was in slow motion, but he did it. When he was through, he had his one egg and toast breakfast.

It didn't take him too long to eat, but while he did, he thought of the dream. With a second

93

cup of coffee and a cigarette in his hand, he went into his office to call the California number Lassiter had given him. Remembering the time difference and how early it was there, he sat in the barber chair and turned on the t.v. instead.

After "Georgey Girl" and water packed tuna fish for lunch and Errol Flynn in "The Adventures of Robin Hood", Hardy placed his call.

Lassiter was no longer registered at the hotel in California. Hardy called the other number Lassiter had given him, the one in Oregon. The female who answered told him that Mr. Lassiter was out of town on business and that she wasn't sure when he would be back.

Her Western accent was pleasant to the ear, "Would you care to leave your name and number?"

"No m'am," said Hardy and he searched the mess on his desk for the puzzle book. Remembering it was in the bedroom, he went to the bookshelf and pulled down an old paperback instead. He skimmed through "Mother Night" until it was time for dinner.

Holmes had ground chuck and cottage cheese, and Hardy had the same.

Anxious as a school boy going to the prom, he shaved and dressed for his second visit to "Fat Limited."

He was very concentrated on where he was and what he expected, still he noticed the man in the gray coat milling about with the others. He seemed so odd and out of place. What was a thin man doing there? Hardy had seen other thin people at "Fat Limited" but these were people you knew had been fat at one time or another. This man was thin and had always been thin and would always be thin . . . there was something familiar about him.

Hardy's thoughts went no further on the subject. They were halted by the jovial representative of "Fat Limited" who was waiting for him to hand over his money.

Hardy paid and went around the corner. He had not weighed himself all week. His eyes riveted to the sign as he walked towards the room and over the mat that concealed the scale: 218.

Three lousy pounds. All that suffering and he had lost only three pounds. Three lousy pounds. Hardy was in no mood to listen to any skinny person giving a lecture on how they used to be fat. He turned at the door and left.

What had happened was distracting, but not so much that he didn't notice gray-coat following him out and then pretending to be interested in some items in a store window. Hardy walked towards him. The man seemed to remember an important engagement elsewhere and took off.

Hardy was doubly sure of his suspicions when he saw that the window his suspected tail had been peering at so intently, held a display of dental equipment. Somehow gray-coat didn't look like the dentist type to Hardy . . . but he did look familiar . . .

The name Marv Leon beeped at him from a hidden memory cell. He was walking now. As he passed a pay phone, he decided to check his service. Gerald Friday had called. Melanie Ryan had called.

He dropped in another dime and dialed Melanie's number. She picked up at the first ring.

"Melanie, it's Pat."

"Pat, a man named Al Ricci called about fifteen minutes ago. He said he wanted to talk to me about something Ben was holding for him and that it could be worth a lot of money to me. Before I could even answer, he said he was coming over right away.

Imprints of the dream he had flickered in his mind.

"Sit tight, Mel, I'll be right there."

Chapter Eight

She was wearing black pants and a yellow silk blouse. Melanie was one of the few women he had ever known that really looked good in pants . . . and without them, a gnawing recollection told him.

"He's not here yet," she said closing the door. "Do you want a drink?"

"Later. When he shows up I want you to talk to him alone. I'll be in the bedroom."

"My favorite room," she answered in a sort of non sequitur, or was it? He looked at her quizzically.

Without warning, she was close to him. "Hold me Pat, hold me tight."

The touch of silk under his hands, the firm

softness of her breasts touching his body, the many exciting odors that she generated and the sound of the buzzer all vied for his attention at the same time.

He ignored the buzzer, but Melanie didn't. She showed that sad smile of hers and went to the house phone. "Yes? . . . thank you."

She crossed back to him. Putting a finger on her lips and then on his, she said, "It's him, he's coming right up."

He reached out his hands and rubbed the silk and the breasts it covered. He could feel her body responding, then she shook her head and giggled, "Get in there, you character."

Hardy snapped his fingers in mock disappointment that was very real and went into the bedroom. There he sat on the bed for a moment with an unlit cigarette in his mouth. Then he pulled the oak side chair away from the wall and up to the door. He waited there, perched on the chair and chewing the filter, until Ricci arrived.

He heard the bell ring and the door open and some words being mumbled. He placed his face close to the almost closed bedroom door.

"Miss Ryan, I realize you don't know me and probably have never heard of me. I'm a very direct and a very sincere person. Ben and I were old friends. Ben was holding . . . this package for me. A package valuable to me and no one else. From what I can gather, it seems to have been mislaid. That's why I'm here. If I could . . ." Here he clapped his hands together several times as if he was thinking of the right word . . . "prevail upon you to work in my behalf and find this package for me, I would be happy to pay you five thousand dollars for your trouble."

"That sounds very interesting, Mr. Ricci . . . could you tell me what's in the package, or what it looks like?"

"Just a package, not too thick, about four inches across and five inches long. Not a very big thing, and five thousand dollars is a very, very fair price."

"I agree," said Melanie, adding a little laugh. "I'll look around and see if I can find it."

Al Ricci's soft voice sounded slightly meaner, "All right, seventy-five hundred, I'm in no mood to fool around."

Hardy opened the bedroom door a bit more.

Melanie was stirring the ice in her drink with her fingers and seemed not at all bothered by Ricci's manner.

"Mr. Ricci, I don't know what you're talking about."

"God damn it, you know exactly what I'm talking about. Ben had the package, Ben's dead. It figures since you were the one closest to him that you have the package. I want it. Ten thousand dollars, that's my last offer."

He moved closer and raised his hand. Melanie

didn't bat an eye. "I'm warning you," he started to say.

Hardy opened the door. "Down tiger, if you're not careful the lady will slap your face and you'll cry and that would be very embarrassing for all of us."

Ricci became spastic in his indecision. He made a fractional move towards Hardy, his hands ready for combat, then his feet turned to the door for flight, then to Melanie, to Hardy and to the door again. Choice made, he ran to the door.

"Come back Al, that's not going to get you anywhere."

Ricci stopped and walked slowly over to the couch wiping his brow with the silk handkerchief as he went. "You're right. Would you happen to have any kirschwasser, I need a drink."

Melanie didn't say anything, but went to the small bar and poured out a healthy portion of the clear colored cherry brandy and gave it to him. Ricci very carefully put his hankerchief away and drank more than half the contents of the glass in one swallow. He pulled out the handkerchief again, dabbed his mouth and returned the square of silk to his pocket.

Between sips of his drink he said, "You very nearly gave me a heart attack, coming out of that room like that . . . that wasn't nice."

Hardy dropped the chewed up cigarette in an

ashtray and lit a fresh one. "And what about what you were planning to do, was that nice?"

"Oh, I never would have hit her. That was just an act. Could I have some more, please."

"Why not?" said Melanie, "Let's have a party. Pat?"

"Scotch," said Hardy. "All right, Al. Why don't you save us all a lot of time by telling us what's in the package."

"No chance," said Ricci.

Hardy was tickled by the way the man shifted his speech patterns, sometimes talking like the fey gay he had become and at other times being the rough talking jock of their college days.

"All right," said Hardy, taking a healthy taste of his scotch. "Tell us what made you think either Melanie or I had it."

"What else could I think after that phony phone call you made. I knew Lassiter put you up to it to make me nervous."

"What does that mean?"

"Never you mind. It got me thinking. I knew where Ben lived, all right. He never let me forget it. After you called me, I called him, but there was no answer. A few days later when I saw in the paper that he was dead, I went to the building, but I saw you and her going in. In a little while I saw you coming out. You have to have it. Who else could?"

"Well," said the detective, "Maybe he had it

101

with him in Mexico. In that case maybe his murderer has it."

Ricci picked at a manicured thumbnail while he thought over what Hardy had said. He stood up and used the handkerchief on his mouth again. "Thank you very much for the drink," and before Melanie or Hardy knew it, he was gone.

They both looked at each other and silently drank their drinks.

Melanie put her empty glass down and said, "What now?"

Hardy thought only briefly of the problems of who killed Ben and of what was in the package and who had it and what everything was really about. Then he thought intently about his own problem and the woman across the room who could help him solve it.

"I have a marvelous idea."

"Oh?"

She sat perfectly still as he crossed the room to her. His hand was moving towards the top button of her silk blouse when they heard the shots. They ran to the window and saw a small crowd gathering around an object that was lying in a heap in the middle of the street. The heap looked like the body of a man.

It was too high up to be sure and the light was bad, but Hardy noticed a familiar form edging away from the crowd and walking slowly towards Fifty-Ninth Street. He kept his eyes on the gray coat and said, "Do you have any binoculars?"

Melanie quickly came up with a pair of opera glasses, but it wasn't quick enough. The man was gone. Nevertheless, Hardy had the funniest of feelings that Marv Leon had just murdered Al Ricci.

The police cars were there before Hardy could pick up the phone. He did anyway and dialed Manhattan North.

"Gerald Friday speaking."

"Hi, it's Pat."

"About time you called me back. You're always bitching about me never keeping you informed. We picked up one of the people you told us about. Vi. It's short for Virginia . . . I don't think it fits her."

"It doesn't."

"She is a very weird person. The only clear cut sentence we have out of her is 'Nirvana is coming on the Fourth of July'. I think I'll turn her over to the Bureau of Narcotics and let them go crazy. The jerky kid had more than five ounces of grass on her when she was picked up."

"Gerry, I hate to bother you, but I think what I have to say is more important."

"You always do, go ahead."

"I am at Melanie Ryan's apartment on Sutton Place. A man named Al Ricci, who went to college with Ben Alsop and me, just left. Shortly after he left, I heard two shots. There is a body

103

in the street, and there are police cars at the scene. To use an old expression that I've heard used recently, I'll bet you dollars to donuts that the body is of one Al Ricci."

"Shit," said the cop, "Every time you're involved life gets complicated . . . besides the fact all three of you went to school together, what's the connection?"

"Come on, City Detective, you don't want me doing all your work for you, do you?" and Hardy hung up the phone, imitating what Friday usually did to him.

Hardy was right, it was Ricci, and by this time the doorman had told the police that he had been visiting Melanie Ryan.

The succeeding time period was spent in answering the same questions many times to different policemen. Definitely not what Hardy had in mind when he told Melanie he had a marvelous idea.

Chapter Nine

When he got home, there were more policemen waiting for him, and a man from the security
company that had installed the alarm system in
his apartment.

The way Hardy time-tabled it, someone had
tried to break into his apartment while he and
Melanie were playing twenty questions with
Homicide. The "someone" had made it past the
front door, but had triggered the alarm when he
had gone to work on the second.

A policeman and the security man had lots of
questions to ask and reports to file, but Hardy's
main concern was getting into the apartment and
placating an hysterical Holmes who was barking
and howling continuously.

When the last stranger had gone and the pandemonium had ceased, Hardy and Holmes were on the chaise.

The poodle had had a dog biscuit, the man, a librium . . . now both were trying to drink from the glass of Irish Mist. He pushed Holmes away and petted him on the head and except for a few vagrant drops, kept all of the brandy for himself.

The movie playing on television was "The Black Swan." It was the only good thing that had happened all day. Hardy watched enviously as Ty Power disposed of the baddies and ended up with Maureen O'Hara in his arms.

On Tuesday with the morning activities out of the way, Hardy spoke to Melanie briefly on the phone and then settled down to do some work. He took the list from the cork wall and crossed out Al Ricci's name and put a big check mark next to Marv Leon's. He hadn't told the police about Leon since it was only a suspicion and not fact . . . but it was a damn strong suspicion . . . and he was pretty sure it was Leon who had made use of his own diversion and tried breaking into the apartment.

He looked at Melanie's name on the list and circled it . . . and then x'd it out completely.

Lassiter? Hardy doodled several question marks around Lassiter's name, but since he wasn't sure where Lassiter was and he was almost positive about Leon, then Marv Leon had to be his next move. He thought about calling Melanie back to see if she had an address on the man, but it occurred to him that he might be Marv Leon's next move and that the best way to flush him out was to go out walking and let Leon find him. The prospect scared the hell out of Hardy, but he knew he was right.

The trouble was, he didn't know why Leon was following him. Did he want the same thing Ricci was after, the package? Or did he have the package and for reasons of his own, would he try to kill him just as he had Ricci?

The more he thought about it, the more Hardy wanted to persuade himself that he was wrong, that the plan was no good. What he needed was a back up man. Steve Macker was out of town and if he tried to get Friday in on this, the cop would tell him to keep his nose out of the City's business. He dialed Jose Hernandez's number. No answer.

After checking in the phone book, he called Hernandez's home. No answer there either. Too bad, he and his brother Manny would be perfect for this sort of job.

The tension was giving him a stomach ache. He went to the kitchen and ate a diet lunch and turned on t.v. and turned off t.v. and tried to read and stopped and had a drink and went to the john and finally went out. He had decided that taking Leon alone was dumb. He would wait a while till he could get some help, but he wasn't going to stay locked up in the house either.

After buying a paper on Broadway, he ambled towards Central Park, and then realizing what he was doing and how perfect a place Central Park was to be ambushed, he took quick looks over his shoulder to be sure he wasn't being followed and darted into the Museum of Natural History.

Inside he rejected the Planetarium as being too dark and got hung up on mental philosophical meanderings when he viewed the Neanderthal Man and the Cro-Magnon Man and compared them to modern man.

He continued in this philosophical vein of thought as he walked west on Seventy-Ninth Street. Had he not been forced into some fancy foot work when he instinctively avoided a clump of messy dog droppings in his path, he might never have noticed Marv Leon, who was still wearing that gray coat.

He had the urge to run, but he didn't know what the hell was on Leon's mind . . . and he would hate to find out in the form of a bullet in his back. As much as he didn't want to, he did the only thing he could do. He waved at the figure on the opposite sidewalk and shouted hello. The man in the gray coat laughed and walked across the street to join him.

"Hello yourself, fatso, . . . hold it. Can't call you that any more. First time I saw you I almost didn't know it was you. You've dropped a lot of weight . . . I guess you've heard what's been happening to a lot of old friends of ours . . . must be a virus or something that's going around."

Marv Leon put his hand on Hardy's arm. "As long as you broke the ice, what do . . ."

Without thinking, Hardy shook the arm off.

"Steady, fatso. Relax. You don't really think you can take me? I mean, just because you lost a few pounds." And without changing his manner or expression, he aimed his stubby fingers at Hardy's throat.

Hardy's mind told his feet to run, but then his mind took its own advice and hid in its own recesses, leaving Hardy and his reflexes all alone. But that was all he needed in a situation like this. The reflexes sent a counter order to the feet to sidestep to the left and another to Hardy's hands to move. And move they did. One chopping at Marv Leon's kidney and another at the back of his neck.

Marv Leon bounced off a car and reached inside his coat. As the gun appeared, Hardy moved in to kick the hand that held it. This time Hardy didn't avoid the dog turds, but slid like a player coming into home plate with the winning run. He heard the shot and the twang of it hitting the lamp post behind him and the sound of one pair of shoes running and of many voices babbling.

When he got up seconds later, Marv Leon was gone and the street seemed as if nothing untoward had happened. The fact of the encounter and the smell of dog crap as he scraped it off his shoe on the curb made him sick. He gagged and threw up his toast and grapefruit and cottage cheese. The sour taste in his mouth didn't make him feel any better. He wiped his mouth with his handkerchief and then he used it to wipe his shoe clean. As he was looking for a place to get rid of the handkerchief, he vomited again.

When he had nothing left, he started a slow walk home. Violence always made him feel ill. The army had made sure that he could cope with it during the fact, but they had never ironed out the wrinkles after the fact.

In the apartment he took two libriums and went to sleep.

It couldn't have been more than several minutes later when he awoke. The pillow was wet with blood. He jumped up . . . and nearly fell down. Ignoring the dizziness, he went to the bathroom. There was blood covering the right side of his face. Hardy turned on both faucets and lowered his face into the basin. He couldn't feel anything and couldn't figure out where he had been hit. He stood up and grabbed blindly at a towel on the rack. Carefully he patted his face until it was dry. He still couldn't feel anything.

Hardy looked at his face in the mirror. There it was. He stared in fascination at the trickle of blood coming from his right ear lobe where Marv Leon's bullet had nicked him.

Dabbing at it with the styptic pencil stung, but it eventually staunched the flow of blood. The damage was less than what could have been inflicted by a nearsighted barber. There was a lousy taste in his mouth. Hardy picked up the mouthwash, put it down, and went into his office for a large scotch. While he sipped, he picked up the phone. He reminded himself in time and switched the phone to his left ear. Hardy tried not to imagine the outcome of the shooting had Leon corrected his windage several inches to the right.

Gerald Friday was on the line, "Yes."

"It's me, Pat."

"There's an individual by the name of Marvin Leon, who also went to school with Ben Alsop and Al Ricci and me."

"What the hell is this, a class reunion?"

"If it is," said Hardy, "we might be holding it at the morgue. Leon just took a shot at me. As soon as I get the other ear pierced, you can buy me earrings for my birthday."

"Cut the comedy, where did this happen?"

"On Seventy-Ninth Street, between Columbus and Amsterdam. One of the light poles on the north side of the street has a slug in it just around the six foot mark. It's probably too mangled to check, but if you get lucky, have it compared to

111

the bullets taken out of Al Ricci, they might match."

"Any ideas why this outbreak is concentrating on your little group?"

Hardy emptied the glass of scotch and savored the taste and feeling. "I might have a good try if you would let me in on why Senor Mendoza is really visiting us from across the Rio Grande."

There was a short silence. Then Friday said, "Be ready in ten minutes. I'll pick you up." And the line was dead.

Hardy changed his clothes and took Holmes' ground chuck out of the freezer to thaw, and was out on the street with a fresh cigarette in his mouth when Friday pulled up. The black cop didn't speak until they were heading downtown on the West Side Highway.

"You probably know that there's a big problem policing the Mexican border. They could never stop stuff coming over when it was strictly on the ground, but now they're flying it in. Small planes that nobody can spot. Not just pot . . . heroin and coke . . . it's a million dollar business. Mendoza figures that maybe your friend Alsop was in on it. Jesus, I never saw such an administrative foul up. Supposedly Mendoza is working on a joint investigation with the Department and with the Federal Bureau of Narcotics and Dangerous Drugs, but everyone is so closed mouth that nothing gets coordinated.

"Homicide is checking to see if Ricci's death

had anything to do with Alsop. I told the precinct to let them know if they got anything out of that lamp post, and I told them you'd be in to give them any extra information they needed."

"Thanks heaps."

"Shut up. Where the hell was I? This case has more curves to it than a snake. Mendoza thinks that Alsop was part of a drug outfit smuggling stuff into the States. He figures he was killed either by unhappy partners or competitors. He figures they were Americans. His investigation seems to tie in with the stuff found on St. Mark's Place and the killing of Al Ricci, and now with this gun happy character Marv Leon, who took a shot at you, and who turns out to be a former business partner of Mr. Alsop . . ."

"Oh yeah," said Hardy, "I forgot to tell you that."

"Private Detective," Friday muttered, "You wouldn't even make a good private boy scout. Back to the point. Up until now ferrying stuff across the border into California or Nevada or New Mexico or Arizona, or where have you, has been pretty much a free lance operation. Lots of free lance operations. Mendoza seems to think that somebody, maybe Alsop, was trying to make one big operation out of it, and that's why he was shot. If Mendoza's right, then Ricci was involved in some way and so is Leon. We'll know more when we nab Leon."

"You mean, *if* you nab Leon. Anything more out of that girl?"

"No. She's out of our hands now. She's in the hospital and some doctors are trying to do something with her. Complete flip out. I think she was on acid or something. I don't know, drugs scare the hell out of me. You ever turn on?"

Hardy looked at Gerald Friday. "Are you putting me on?"

"I'm asking you a straight question. Did you ever turn on?"

"Who's asking. Gerald Friday or Detective Gerald Friday?"

"I ought to throw you out of the goddam car. Just answer the question."

Hardy didn't believe that Friday was as naive as he seemed but he answered the question. "Yes."

They were coming down the off ramp. Friday pulled over and parked. "Why?"

"You've got to be kidding," said Hardy. "A little pot never hurt anybody."

"Now *you've* got to be kidding," said Friday, "I grew up with guys who started with a little pot and then went to a little sniffing and then a little shooting up and most of those clowns are dead or wish they were."

Friday started up the car again and drove towards midtown. After a while he said, "Where do you want me to let you off?"

"I don't get it," said Hardy, "I thought we were going somewhere?"

"Nope, just thought I'd fill you in, and I didn't want anyone else to know about it. Who knows, you might get lucky. And if you do, that would mean I could get off of the crumby detail and Mendoza would go home and the Federal people would go back to whatever it is they do, and I could get back to my own job. I've got a lot of paperwork that needs catching up on, and nobody is doing it for me while I'm on this special assignment. You've got the right angle, Pat. Someday I'm going to turn in my badge and become a 'private detective' and lead the good life."

"Shit," said Hardy, "Let me off here."

Here was in front of a frankfurter stand.

"One more thing," said Friday, "Mendoza is very suspicious of your connection with Alsop. He figures that you might even be involved in this drug racket. Hasta luego." And he was gone.

Hardy mulled over what Friday had said, especially Mendoza's suspicions. He laughed out loud. Then self-consciously he looked around. Nobody was paying any attention to him. He ate two franks and drank a coke while he enjoyed all the pretty sweatered breasts that went bouncing by.

Finished eating, he went to see a double feature. It was evening when he came out of the movie house and had a cab take him to the precinct. There he told the desk sergeant what had happened earlier that day. The sergeant looked pained when Hardy told him how many hours ago it had all happened. Hardy explained that he had notified Manhattan North earlier, but the man's expression didn't change. Hardy shrugged and left.

He walked home trying to figure Friday out. He couldn't.

While Holmes ate his chuck, Hardy dined on meatloaf and tomato. Dinner finished, he phoned Melanie. No answer. He dialed his service. Melanie had called him earlier. Hardy was bothered that he had missed her, but not too much. He wasn't really up to anything, including Melanie. He picked up the 'TV Guide' to see what was on that night.

Chapter Ten

The next day Hardy tried to pretend there was no problem and no case and no nothing. He listened to Duke Ellington records and read. The trouble was that certain portions of his mind kept at it even while the rest of him was goofing off.

Camus depressed him. Hardy put the old paperback down and picked up a new book that Ruby had given him, "They Eat Their Young," by George and Gladys Spelven. It was a show business novel, and Hardy was pleased to see that he was able to recognize some friends. In the first chapter he spotted Hollywood sexpot Susannah Dow immediately.

Hardy chuckled when he read the line describing Susannah as trisexual—she would try anything. He had met the actress while working on another case and the description was true. Regretfully Hardy put the new book aside and thought about his case. He lit a cigarette. Betsy . . . he would have to find Betsy. She wasn't a great lead, but she was the only one he had. He parked the new book on the table by the barber chair for later reading and then wrote Betsy's name on the list without even bothering to take it from the cork wall.

He sat back down at his desk and rubbed at the places on his face he had missed when shaving. He looked up to see Holmes' soulful gaze.

"Stop staring at me, you crazy animal."

The dog wagged his tail and came over and licked Hardy's hand. Hardy scratched the poodle behind the ear and leaned back in his chair. He didn't feel like doing a damn thing. With a surge of effort he sat up and reached for the phone and dialed Jose Hernandez's number.

"Hernandez speaking."

"Jose?"

"Yes."

"This is Pat Hardy."

"Hello, what can I do for you?"

"You know the apartment on St. Mark's Place where they had the fire and the police found all that pot?"

"I heard about it."

"It was a crash pad. A girl named Betsy lived there, also a weirdo type called Jack. I was wondering if you would nose around down there and see if you can get a line on either one of them."

"Sounds simple enough. Give me what you have on them."

Hardy described Betsy and Jack and Hernandez said he would get right on it.

With the phone call out of the way, Hardy's energy was depleted. He leaned back in the chair again and looked at the ceiling. He yawned, looked at his watch and then at the ceiling again. He was just nodding off when the phone rang.

" 'Trouble Limited', Patrick Hardy speaking."

"Now that sounds impressive. Pat, you old son of a bitch, I am really impressed."

Another country heard from, George Lassiter.

"Hello, George."

"I'm impressed again. Second time in all these years that you've heard my voice, and you recognized me just like that. Tell you what, I'm in town, and I thought the two of us might get together. Hoist a few and talk over old times. Let's have dinner. I'm at the Regal. Why don't you meet me here about six o'clock. What do you say?"

"Sure thing," said Hardy, "The Regal. Six o'clock."

He hung up the phone. Common sense told him that Lassiter had to be in this thing up to his neck. He still couldn't put the pieces of the puzzle together though. Who were the cowboys and

119

who were the Indians? Maybe after dinner he would know.

The Regal. That was where Peg had stayed. After all this time, he still couldn't get Peg Robbins out of his mind. She was nude the last time he had seen her. He remembered that even in passion she was vain. In the midst of love he had told her she was beautiful and even as she turned and twisted in the act of sex, she preened at what he had said and made her flat stomach flatter and thrust her high breasts higher. It was the best he had ever known. In his memory Sara Vaughan was singing, and he was lying next to Peg, admiring the lovely blue veins in her breasts.

Hardy opened his eyes and made a noise. Holmes, startled, looked at him warily.

"Nonsense," said Hardy getting up and stretching. He went to the kitchen to get Holmes' food ready and soothed his own stomach with several slices of toast and a cup of tea.

The cab dropped him in front of the Regal Hotel shortly after six. When he asked for George Lassiter's room, he was directed to a housephone. He asked the question again of the operator.

"One moment, please," and he heard her ring the room.

"Hello."

"Hello, George. Pat."

"Come on up. We'll have a drink first before we eat. I'm in 1242."

120

As he rode up on the self-service elevator, Hardy's memory kept drifting back to school and the five of them. First it had been the three of them, and then it was the five of them. Funny how it all happened after . . .

"Going down?" The woman entered the elevator and then looked annoyed glances at Hardy for not warning her that the car was going up. At twelve he smiled apologetically and got off.

The arrowed sign pointed down the hall. 1242. He rang the bell.

"It's open. Come on in."

George Lassiter was tying his necktie. He looked pretty much the way Hardy expected him to. The same, just older.

"Son of a bitch, if you don't beat all. Pat, you look great. When'd you lose all that lard? Never mind. Pour us both a drink. Scotch for me. This country boy has picked up some city habits. Remember when I used to say scotch was for fairies and that the only drink for a man was sour mash? The good old days. That's what we call 'em, don't we? Bull, these are the good old days! 'Live fast, die young, have a good looking corpse.' What's that from?"

Hardy's lips were dry, the room was too warm. "A book, 'Knock on Any Door'," he answered as he poured the drinks.

"Dollars to donuts you'd know that. If it comes from a book, ask Pat Hardy. How the hell you been, you old son of a bitch?"

121

Hardy was a bit thrown by this Rotary Club greeting. He hadn't remembered George Lassiter as that much of a hick.

"Pretty good, George, pretty good. You heard about Ben?"

"Yeah, ain't it a shame? The pity is maybe I could have saved his life if your wire had come just a little sooner. I found out where he was staying in L.A. and just missed him. Not a half hour before I got there he had taken off . . . and Al too. I heard that Al got killed. Sure is a coincidence."

Hardy was about to say something about Marv Leon but kept quiet. Lassiter had his jacket on now. "Over the lips, past the gums, look out stomach, here she comes." He drained the glass. "Come on, Pat, drink up, we got some partying to do. You know you never did send me a bill for your work. I'll just have to make it up to you."

Hardy tossed off his drink and followed Lassiter out the door. On the elevator Lassiter regaled him with the same stories he had told Hardy two weeks earlier when he had called from L.A.

"Wait till you taste this steak. Wouldn't believe it if I hadn't tried it myself, but this little hotel dining room has the best steak in New York, not like back home of course, but damn good for New York."

Several more drinks and the promised steaks

arrived. They were good. Hardy had doubles of everything.

"How do you put it away and stay thin?" Lassiter inquired.

Hardy grinned and kept eating.

When they had finished their ice cream and were having coffee and cigarettes, Lassiter beamed at the two women coming through the entrance and checked his watch. "That's what I call perfect timing." Lassiter rose in his chair and waved the girls over. "Something special I arranged."

Despite himself and the situation, Hardy had enjoyed the first part of the evening and now was looking forward to the rest of it. Joyce and Connie were introduced rather vaguely by Lassiter, and they joined the two men at the table.

Hardy found himself paired off with Joyce as they all bundled into a cab. He was glad. Joyce had the larger bosom and her hand rested on his crotch every chance it got. The small portion of his brain that was functioning with any clarity knew that the girls were hookers, classy looking, but hookers. Hardy didn't care. That small portion also knew that Lassiter was trying to con him into something. Again he didn't care. As they went from bar to bar, all that was on Hardy's mind was the expectation of Joyce's naked body in bed with his.

Things happened as he expected. Memories of bed and anticipation, and naked bodies and bouncing breasts, and anticipation and friction, and sweat and perfume, and climax and sweet sleep all combined as someone roughly shook him awake.

"All right, lover boy, fun's over. Time to wake up."

Hardy forced his eyes open. Joyce or Connie or whatever her name was, was gone. George Lassiter, wearing a robe and smoking a cigarette and drinking a bottle of beer, was doing the shaking.

"I'm up, I'm up," Hardy protested, 'Where's the fire?"

"No fire. Just wanted to talk."

"Now? . . . Where's the girls?"

"Forget them, you jerk, let's talk."

"Give me a cigarette . . . thanks," said Hardy, inhaling and coughing the smoke, "I needed that. All right. What do we talk about?"

"We talk about a package that Ben Alsop had."

Hardy yawned and rubbed his eyes. "Excuse me. You know, I wondered when that subject would come up."

"Well, it's come up. I want the package."

"Sounds fair enough," said Hardy. "Why didn't you come straight out with it? Why drinks and dinner and girls and everything . . . I'm not saying I minded, but why bother?"

Lassiter put down the empty beer bottle. "For years I've been selling feed and grain and machinery and making deals, and no matter what the business was, it never hurt to give the customer . . . or the seller a good time up front. It always helped the deal along. All right, the fun time is over, now to business. You've got the package, I want it. How much?"

"Just like that, huh?"

"What do you mean, just like that?" said Lassiter. "Don't try any double talk . . . have you made a deal with Marv Leon?"

"Hell, no," said Hardy, "He took a shot at me."

"Well, there you have it. You know where you stand with a maniac like that . . . with me it's pure profit. Twenty-five thousand dollars, payable on delivery, no questions asked."

Hardy dragged on his cigarette, "Very generous offer."

"Don't forget, Pat, I could go the other route. You rile me and I'll beat the crap out of you, and I'm the one who can do it, you know that."

The talk was making Hardy very nervous. He had been afraid of Lassiter back in school, and he was afraid of him now. Suddenly he had to urinate. He pushed the blanket away to get out of the bed.

"God damn it, you bastard, pay attention when I talk to you." With this, Lassiter started a backhand across Hardy's face.

Hardy rolled away from the hand and out of the bed into a ready position, his reflexes ready to take Lassiter on, even if he wasn't. Unfortunately, his reflexes didn't take into account his body chemistry. As his feet hit the floor and his hands prepared to fight, another dizzy spell occurred. Lassiter's left hand flicked out. Hardy leaned away from it and kept leaning. He was falling even before Lassiter hit him with the combination.

He could hear Lassiter mumbling as he hit him. "I never liked you. Always stuffing your face, and those God damn books . . . Alsop, I didn't like him either. Always clicking away with those God damn cameras and always doing those stupid puzzles . . . intellectuals . . . Christ, you two made me sick."

The words were only a background for the flailing fists that were not doing Hardy any good. Mercifully he passed out.

When he awoke this time, it was with memories of pain and sour spit in his mouth. Hardy opened his eyes to see Lassiter sitting patiently.

"Welcome back. You're a disappointment to me, Pat. When you jumped like that I thought at least the years had made a man out of you. I didn't even work up a sweat. You're a pushover . . . I have to admit you did make a try. That's more than the old Pat Hardy would have done. Who knows, another fifteen, twenty years, you might be all there."

Hardy swallowed several times in order not to throw up. "What happens now?"

"Nothing. Get out. You don't have the package. If you did, I'd have gotten it out of you by now. That colored girl has it. I'll get it from her."

Hardy got into his clothes as fast as possible, his brain racing, trying to evaluate the situation. He shoved his tie into his pocket and laced up his shoes. "Wrong, George, I do have it."

"Then what the hell was this all about?"

"Just playing hard to get," Hardy touched his puffed up lip tenderly, "I guess I played too hard for my own good."

Lassiter stood up, his arms akimbo, ready to lash out again. "Prove it."

"I'll tell you what. You pay me for the proof. One thousand dollars. Then, in one week, when I deliver the package, you pay me another fifty thousand dollars. Also, you promise to stay clear of me and that girl during this week and from then on. Deal?"

"Why a week? And what's with you and that nigger? You getting a taste for dark meat?"

"It'll take a week because it will take a week, and never mind about the rest of it."

"Let's hear the proof."

Hardy recollected Al Ricci's description of the package and repeated it for Lassiter. "It's just a package, not too thick, about four inches across and five inches long."

"That's it?" asked Lassiter.

"That's a thousand dollars worth. How about it?"

127

Lassiter went to his coat and pulled out a bill-fold. He peeled off some bills and gave them to Hardy. "There's five hundred dollars. You have five days. Monday night, you have the package, and I'll pay you thirty-four thousand five for a total payment of thirty-five thousand dollars. I'll call you. If you're playing games with me, I'll kill you. Get out."

Hardy shoved the money in his coat and left. Alone in the elevator, he looked at his battered reflection in the mirror. "What the hell was that all about?"

The reflection didn't have the answer either.

Chapter Eleven

Merle Doyle stepped back to appraise her work. None of **Hardy's** cuts needed stitches, but it had taken an assortment of bandaids to keep his face from leaking blood. She shook her head at the effect. "I may just put in a revolving door for you."

Hardy tried to smile, but his swollen lip wouldn't let him. "Save the remarks if you don't mind. Another thing, you have to do something about that medication. I'm not in the kind of work where I can keep getting dizzy spells like an old lady. This last one nearly got me killed."

"And if you don't take it, that may kill you," she answered, "So you're damned if you do and damned if you don't. I'll take your pressure and let you know."

The attractive doctor took Hardy's blood pressure several times. When she was finished, she said, "You are the most contrary man in the universe. Now when I expect your pressure to be soaring, it's down in the absolute cellar. Who knows, maybe excitement calms you down? Maybe what you need is a life full of crisis. Okay, cut down to one and a half pills a day, but no less. Fifteen milligrams is as low as I want you to go."

"Thank you, M'am."

"And let your dentist check you over," she said as she walked into her office.

Hardy trailed behind her taking the moment to enjoy the movement of her ass under her white coat. She turned up the volume of the Brahm's Piano Concerto on the radio.

"I'm sorry," said Hardy, "I didn't hear what you said."

"Go see your dentist. Some of your teeth might be loose, or is that sound I hear your brain rattling around in your head."

"Whatever happened to the doctor who used to pat the patient on the head and say, 'there there, it'll be better soon'?"

"You don't want a doctor, you want a mother."

"That's not exactly my secret fantasy about you."

Merle Doyle smiled, "Get the hell out of here. Your pressure's fine. I want to see you in about a month to see how it's doing."

Hardy tried to smile back and winced at the pain. He waved and left the office.

His dentist, Sebastian Lee, put some foul tasting purple stuff on his gums and told him to eat soft food for several days.

"That's great, between you and my doctor, all that's left for me is dietetic baby food."

Out on the street again, he tried to put things in some sort of perspective. Lassiter had given him five days and with the morning already gone, that meant just four and a half left, and he didn't have the vaguest idea as to where that package was. He didn't even know what the package was. It was too small to contain any great amount of dope, it might not even have anything to do with dope.

The more he thought about it, he was pretty sure that Lassiter had killed Ben Alsop or had been close by when it had happened. Maybe Lassiter and Leon were working together.

As this last thought filtered through, Hardy looked about just to make sure that Marv Leon wasn't behind him. Less than satisfied with his safety, he took a cab home.

It was Thursday and he had left the apartment before Laura had arrived. He wasn't relishing the comments she would make about his beat up face.

Holmes barked him in.

"That's enough, Holmes. Hello Laura," and he tried to rush into his office.

"Good Lord, Mr. Hardy. What on earth happened to your face?"

"Nothing, just a run in with my friendly neighborhood mugger."

"You too? It's getting so a person isn't safe walking the streets these days. Your service called." And clucking her tongue, she went back to work.

He dialed his answering service and they told him that a Mr. Hernandez had called. Hardy looked up Jose Hernandez's number and called it.

"Jose?"

"No, it's Manny. Who's this?"

"Pat Hardy."

"Good. Jose told me to call you. He thinks he found your friend Betsy. You know where Allen and Broome Street is?"

"Yes."

"Meet him on the corner there as soon as you can."

"Right."

"Do you want me there, too?" asked Manny.

"Was she alone?"

"That's right. Jose says she's the only one in the place as far as he can tell."

"Then I guess he and I can handle it. Thanks a lot."

"Okay," said Manny, "So long."

As he hung up Hardy noticed that his shirt was wet with sweat. He started for the bedroom to change it when he realized that it might be his last chance to eat for a while. Laura was in the kitchen polishing the set of silver that once belonged to Hardy's parents and that he used only on rare occasions.

"Laura, put some water up and make me a cup of bouillon please, and put out a banana."

"That's not enough for you to eat," she told his back as he went to change.

He chuggalugged the soup and stuffed the banana into his pocket while Laura chided him about not getting enough to eat and Holmes danced around in the expectation that he was going out for a trip to the park. When Hardy left without him, Holmes yapped angrily while Laura egged the poodle on.

Hardy decided the subway would be faster than a cab. As he got on the train, he realized he still had the five hundred dollars Lassiter had given him. All that Hardy could think of as he ate his banana was that as soon as he entered the Lower East Side, someone would really mug him and relieve him of the five hundred dollars. Surreptitiously, he shoved the bills into his shoe.

On Delancy Street he bought a frankfurter and munched while he headed towards the corner of Broome and Allen.

"Hardy?"

Only as he turned to acknowledge his name did he remember that he had never met Jose Hernandez even though the man had worked for him on several occasions before.

They shook hands silently as Hardy examined the short well built man. The smiling face reminded him of what he himself looked like at the moment. "How did you know who I was?"

"When you live down here you get to know who belongs and who doesn't. I have to admit, with those lumps, I wasn't too sure for a minute. How does the other guy look?"

Hardy made a face. "Too good to talk about it. What's with the girl?"

"That building over there, with the broken stoop. Some kid I know tagged her for me. He was playing up there on the bridge when he saw her walking over from Brooklyn . . . she's coming out. What do we do?"

Hardy closed his eyes for a second. "Nobody else up there, right?"

"That's it."

'Okay," said Hardy, "You check the room out. I'll take her. Talk to you later."

Hernandez nodded, and they went their separate ways. Betsy led him back to Delancy Street and up the stairs to the pedestrian walk on the Williamsburgh Bridge. He wondered what strange fascination Brooklyn had for the girl as he tailed her bouncy ass across. It was a nice day. Just enough people so Betsy wouldn't notice

him and not too many to make following her
difficult. He smiled a lot as the rear image of her
triggered memory tapes of them thrashing
around over burlap together.

He got so caught up that he didn't notice
that Betsy had stopped to look down at the water.
When Betsy started again, he gave her a bit of a
lead before following again. As he did, he had the
strangest feeling on the back of his neck. He
never had the chance to get curious about it.
Just at that moment he heard his name being
called. "Hardy, look out."

He flattened himself on the concrete surface.
The girl started running. The bullets made two
sounds: the explosive noise when they left the
gun and the pinging one as they tore grooves
into the concrete near his head.

People were screaming. Hardy felt that whoever was firing had him zeroed in and would get
him any second. Not wanting to wait around to
see if his hunch was right, he dove for the pro-
tective covering of a trash basket several feet
away. Hardy looked back to see Marv Leon
standing on a bench and holding his gun in two
hands and aiming it right at him.

Quiet as the grave was the thought that went
through his head as he watched Leon put pressure on the trigger. Hardy started the movement
that would take him out of the line of fire. He
wondered if he would make it or would he be
dead in the next second. He heard the shot. Then

with an almost academic detachment, he watched Marv Leon stagger and slump and then fell off the bench. Hardy moved his eyes in a fast arc. There was Jose Hernandez ready to let loose another slug at Marv Leon, but one had been enough.

Hardy got to his feet and wiped the gray grit from his hands on his pants. He crossed over to the Spanish detective who was reholstering his gun.

"Gracias, amigo," said Hardy.

Hernandez gave him a cigarette. "For nothing."

"That's what you say . . . you got a match?"

Hernandez lit them both up, and they sat on another bench waiting for the men of the Seventh Precinct to come up on the bridge to see what all the shooting was about.

While the police did their job, Hernandez filled Hardy in.

"When I got up to the girl's apartment, I looked out the window and saw this guy latch onto you while you were following the girl. Don't you ever look back when you're following somebody? You could have had a platoon on your back and you wouldn't have known it."

Hardy smiled sheepishly. "I usually do . . . I was distracted."

Hernandez smiled back without humor and shook his head. "That kind of distraction could get you killed one of these days . . . don't you carry a gun?"

"Nope. Might hurt myself . . . but I'm glad you do."

"Maybe you're right at that. I'm going to get a lot of hassling over plugging that guy . . . they don't like it when you misuse a privilege," and he patted his empty holster.

"Relax, Jose, he killed one person that I know of."

"That's good. When it's someone they want dead, it's not too bad . . . anyway, I ran out of that apartment and after you . . . I caught up on Delancy Street. Man, it was like a line, the girl in front and the rest of us following. I figured on a tour of Brooklyn when that jerk pulled out his gun and went after you. Right in the middle of all those people. He must have been crazy."

At the station, while the detectives were asking Hernandez some more questions, Hardy asked if a call to Detective Gerald Friday would be considered his one call.

"Don't be a wise guy. What's Gerry Friday got to do with this?"

His interrogator was a gruff detective with close cropped gray hair and an unlit cigar hanging out of his mouth.

"Well," said Hardy, "the dead man is wanted for murder and attempted murder on the Upper West Side. My name is Patrick Hardy and . . ."

"Shit . . . Friday told me all about you. My name's Al Gold. Gerry's a friend of mine, I broke him in. He told me about you. Says you're a pain in the ass, but sometimes you get lucky."

Hardy laughed. "That about sums it up."

Gold chewed on his cigar. "Fill me in on this thing."

Hardy started back with Ben Alsop getting killed in Mexico and told the whole story. When he was through, Gold put through a call to Friday and spoke to him.

Fifteen minutes later Hardy and Hernandez were out on the street again. Jose was bitching about how long it was going to take to get his gun back and all the red tape he would have to go through. Hardy leaned against the outside of the building and took off his shoe. "So far all I've made on this case is five hundred bucks. Here's two hundred for you."

"Okay," said Hernandez, "If that's all you think your life's worth."

"Come on Jose, don't con me."

"Who's conning? I was just stating the facts."

Hardy put up his right hand in a halt signal. "All right, con job over, you win. You have fifty bucks change?"

Hernandez looked pained.

"What did you expect?" said Hardy, "the whole hundred? Give me fifty."

They exchanged bills and Hardy said, "There,

138

two fifty for me and two fifty for you, even split. Thanks again. Adios."

"Right," said Hernandez, grinning broadly. "See you around."

Chapter Twelve

At home Hardy put out Holmes' food, prepared a peanut butter sandwich and a glass of milk for himself and called Gerald Friday.

"I've been expecting you to call . . . you know of more ways of getting into trouble."

"What are you complaining about?" said Hardy through a mouthful of peanut butter. "I've eliminated one of your cast of characters, haven't I? Makes it less complicated."

"Don't be so cute. You're lucky Gold was there and that he's a friend of mine . . . hell, if you had walked another hundred yards before everything happened, the Brooklyn cops would have you, and you'd probably still be there. Be glad for the little favors life throws your way."

"On that note of philosophy I will hang up and puke."

"Screw you," said Friday, and was gone.

Hardy picked up "They Eat Their Young" again, but he was in no mood for it. Camus didn't appeal to him either. He wandered into the living room and turned on the t.v. and sat on the couch. Holmes jumped up and demanded attention. He ignored the dog and finished his snack and watched Bogart make everyone else jump through the hoop. While he watched, Hardy did in two tomatoes and a can of tuna fish and the rest of the milk. He fell asleep just as Bogie was telling Mary Astor that he wouldn't play the sap for her.

When he woke up, he had an awful taste in his mouth. Tuna fish and milk was not the best thing to eat before going to sleep. The t.v. was still on. Hardy turned off the set and lit a cigarette. He wandered aimlessly around the room trying to come fully awake. He picked up the crossword puzzle book which Laura had placed on the coffee table. No matter where he left things, Laura was always sure to put them some place else. He went to his office to get a pencil and sat in the barber chair yawning and puzzle solving. Holmes wandered in, blinked his eyes a few times and jumped up on the chaise and went to sleep.

When Hardy finished all the puzzles in the book, he glanced through those in the front that

Ben had done. Having nothing better to amuse himself with, he decided to check his skill against Ben's and mentally redo those already done. Demon. Agamemnon. Granulate.

It occurred to him that there was something funny about the words Ben had left out, the ones he himself had filled in that first day in Ben's Madison Avenue apartment while Melanie was busy searching. There wasn't any sense in their being left out. Hardy thumbed ahead and found two more. All were horizontal words, but even if Ben hadn't known them, all he had to do was finish filling in the corresponding vertical words which he obviously knew . . . the spaces had been left blank deliberately . . .

Hardy jotted down the omitted words, there were only four of them: daguerrotype, below, federal, cabinet.

"The picture is below the Federal cabinet," he said out loud.

Holmes looked up, saw it wasn't meant for him and went back to sleep.

Hardy started singing a made up song. "The package with the picture is beneath the Federal cabinet. The cabinet with the eagle is in Melanie's room."

He dialed the phone while he sang the song and while he remembered that he had never looked for the package at all in Melanie's apartment because he had figured whoever had torn the apartment apart would have found it. But what if that was what he was meant to think?

"Hello."

"Hi, it's me, Pat."

"Oh, I'm so glad you called. I've been sitting here waiting. Has anything happened?"

"You poor kid. If you were so worried, why didn't you call me?"

"To tell you the truth, I didn't want to bug you. Is anything new?"

"Yeah, I'll be right over to tell you about it."

Hardy hung up the phone and lit a cigarette. The package with the picture or pictures had probably been there all the time where Ben had placed it under the Federal secretary in Melanie's bedroom. The question was, did Melanie know about it? More questions followed. Was she holing out on him? Why? What sort of pictures?

He smoked another cigarette.

And two more in the cab to Sutton Place.

"Come on in," Melanie said. She was wearing a bright red dressing gown, the same one she had been clutching in her hand only a week before. The picture of her nude body processed through his brain.

"Hi," he said inanely.

"You want a drink?"

"Sure." He lit a new cigarette while he waited for her to pour the scotch. "Thanks . . . Melanie, tell me about you and Ben."

"What do you mean?" she asked as she sat in one of the wicker chairs.

He took a long drink of scotch. The whisky took the tuna fish taste away. "How long?"

"A little more than four years. He had a coffee shop then. He hired me to work the cash register. The first day he came on, we clicked, and I moved in with him the next week."

"Was Marv Leon around then?"

"Marv was always around, which was a funny thing . . ."

"What do you mean?" said Hardy.

"Any deal that Ben went into he took Marv along, and I mean took, because he didn't need him, not at all, except maybe as a stooge who said yes when Ben wanted to hear it. Most people thought they were buddies . . . not true, he and Marv hated each other's guts."

"Then why did they stick together?"

"Search me. Anyway, they sold the coffee shop a couple of years ago and bought the health food store. A few months ago he and Marv had a fight and split up, and Ben made me his partner."

"What did they fight about?"

"I don't know, but they both got very mean."

Hardy refilled his glass with booze and ice and in the most matter of fact tone asked, "Did you ever see the pictures?"

"What?"

145

"The pictures, the pictures in the package. Did you ever see them?"

"No. Is that what's in the package, pictures?"

"Yeah. Come on. Let's go in the bedroom."

Melanie laughed. "I like that. Your technique is a little abrupt, but I like that, too."

Hardy put the cold glass to his forehead as he walked into the other room. That would be the best thing, forget about the stupid package and get into bed with Melanie. He was about to turn around and suggest it when she said, "Wait a minute . . . I must be getting slow. You acted as if I knew about the pictures. What was it, a trick question? Is that the bit? I've known about the pictures from the beginning and I've been stringing you along? So Pat Hardy, the big deal detective, sets me up and down I come with the wrong answer. I let slip that I knew about the pictures and you have me in a corner and I confess all. Is that it? I'm waiting for an answer."

"Something like that."

"Go away, Pat. Please go away."

"Mel, I'm sorry . . ."

"Get out, get out, get out."

Her eyes were burning with anger. Hardy pulled her to him and kissed her. His lip was still sensitive where Lassiter had hit him. He was starting not to notice it when Melanie, still angry, bit him. Hardy jumped back in pain.

"Pat . . . I'm sorry, I didn't mean it. Are you all right?"

He touched his lip with his finger to satisfy himself that it wasn't bleeding. "I think so."

Gently Melanie kissed the sore spot, then she kissed him all over the face. "I'm sorry, I guess I'm on edge."

"That's all right, baby." He was caressing her neck and wondering how to open the robe when she said, "What pictures?"

"Later."

"What pictures?"

"Under the secretary."

Melanie ran to the secretary and peered under it. "Where?"

Her rump was sticking up in the air. He didn't know whether he wanted to kick it or grab it. "Here, let me look."

A half hour later they still hadn't found any pictures. Melanie ran her fingers through her hair and said to him, "Wrong."

"I guess so," he answered. He looked at her and then at the eagle atop the secretary. Neither had the answer. Or if they had, they weren't telling. Hardy closed his eyes and thought about Ben's letter: "The proof is

my apartment."

He started chanting different combinations. "The proof is in my apartment. The proof is near my apartment. The proof is under something near my apartment. The proof is under the Federal cabinet near my apartment."

And he looked at the eagle on the secretary

147

again, only this time he imagined it with the inscription "U.S. Mail" beneath it.

"That's got to be it," he said and he kissed Melanie and ran for the door.

"What?" she demanded.

Hardy didn't answer. Instead he came back and gave her his house keys. "Do me a favor, I think I can wrap this up. I forgot to feed Holmes. You go home and feed him and then when I get there I'll tell you all about it and we can celebrate in the best way I know how."

"First you tell me what the hell this is all about."

"Pay no attention to the numbers on the keys, that's just to confuse people. One is two and two is three . . . three is one."

"Shove your stupid keys. Will you please tell me what the hell you are talking about?"

"One question, Melanie sweetheart, is there or isn't there a mailbox on the corner downstairs from Ben's apartment?"

"I think so. No, I know so. There is."

"Well, that's it. A mailbox could also be called a Federal cabinet. Goodbye."

Melanie followed him to the door. "What the hell does that mean?"

Hardy pushed the elevator button and whistled nervously.

"Pat, what does that mean?"

The elevator arrived. He smiled and waved and said, "I'll explain it all later. Goodbye."

Chapter Thirteen

Hardy told the driver Ben Alsop's address and was about to get into the cab when he remembered what Jose Hernandez had said. He looked around and checked the street behind him. He wondered about the dark blue Buick but didn't dwell on it. Three blocks later when he turned around to check again, the Buick was right behind.

"Driver, forget what I told you, just drive around for a while." While he spoke Hardy fished out a five and dropped it in the money tray. He had just decided it could only be Lassiter when the cab stopped for a red light. Hardy waited for the light to change back. As it did and as the driver's foot left the brake,

Hardy left the cab. He hoped the driver wouldn't notice his absence for a couple of blocks. He ran down a dark block and found another cab.

"Where to?"

Hardy told him and lit a cigarette and settled back to enjoy the ride.

Once there, he told the cabbie to pull in close to the corner and wait. Luckily there were no cars in the space. Hardy got out of the taxi, knelt down to tie his shoe and reached under the mailbox. It was there, secured to the underside by magnets. He tugged it free. It was a slim package wrapped in thick gray paper. Hardy shoved the package into his pocket as he stood up and got back into the cab.

The opposite door was open.

"Hi, old buddy. Imagine meeting you here. How about a lift back to my hotel?"

It was George Lassiter.

Lassiter was sitting next to him now. "Do as I tell you, Pat, or you're in trouble," he whispered. "If you play it the way I call it, you could walk away from this whole thing."

Hardy nodded and told the driver to take them to the Regal.

"How did you get here?" Hardy asked. "I thought I ditched you ten minutes ago."

Lassiter bellowed out a laugh. "That wasn't me you ditched. I don't know who it was, but it wasn't me. I've been on you since Thursday. I even saw what happened on the bridge . . .

it's a good thing for me you had someone watching your back . . . Marvin nearly blew blew the whole thing for me then and there . . . you got someone watching your back now?"

Lassiter looked around. "No, I thought not. Not smart enough. I followed you to that colored girl's building. I was not ten feet away when you got into that cab and told him to go to Ben's place. I knew you weren't smart enough to lay a false trail so I lit out and was ahead of you on Madison Avenue and waited for you to find the whole kit and kaboodle for me, and you did. I've been ahead of you all the way . . . I'll take the package now, Pat."

"What's in it?"

"You don't want to know that. Give me the package."

"Wait a minute, George. There's the little matter of my fee."

Lassiter laughed. "Pat, you tickle me, you really do. You sure have picked up a lot of gumption since school. You're right. We made a deal. You come upstairs with me and I'll pay you off."

They were at the hotel. Hardy went through the revolving door with the thought of jamming the door and leaving Lassiter trapped. Lassiter smiled slightly as if he knew what was on Hardy's mind and went through the adjoining door,

151

coming out abreast of Hardy. "The elevator's this way, Pat."

"I . . . need a pack of cigarettes."

"I have plenty upstairs."

"Right."

On the elevator and in the hall, Hardy kept looking for his chance. It never happened. In the room Lassiter said, "Pour us both a drink. We need it. I know I do. It's been a long haul . . . almost twenty years."

"What do you mean?"

"Never you mind. Here's your money. Give me the pictures and get out."

Hardy knew he should do just that. He didn't.

"You know George, I've always been a curious person. After all I've been though to get these pictures, I'd like to take a look at them."

"Curiosity killed the cat, Pat. That's from a book I read once." He gulped down a swallow of scotch. "The more I think about it, the more I know I can't let you leave here anyway. Look at the pictures, Pat, and then think about how it's going to feel to fall out of a twelfth floor window . . . goddamn it, look at them! You said you wanted to . . ." His voice was mean, the way Pat remembered it "Do it!"

Hardy could feel the pulse in his temple throbbing. His heart was beating a mile a minute, and he knew his blood pressure was zooming higher each second that passed. His stomach ached and his bowels were churning with fear.

"Look at them."

Hardy tore away the gray paper. There were about a dozen photos packed between several pieces of cardboard.

"You like to look at pictures, Pat, these are beauties. Lot of money in pictures. Out of my pocket into Ben's. All those years. Then he stopped and I figured it was over, but when he was short of money, he started up again. I couldn't live with that a second time. That's when I decided to kill him. But the sneaky bastard didn't have them with him . . . why do you think we put up with him or with you for that matter? Those goddamn pictures . . . all those years, bleeding me. And for what? For a no good tramp. For a gang bang with a no good tramp. He squeezed Al for all he could, too. Marv didn't have anything so Ben made him hang around and be his stooge. He even made Marv some money so he could take it away from him. Ben was sick . . . that man was sick . . he deserved to die. Look at the pictures, damn you!"

Hardy looked. The poses were all very similar. All of George Lassiter and Al Ricci and Marv Leon in a wooded area in the act of raping or striking a girl. Hardy remembered . . . the girl who was reported missing that year . . she was never found.

"That's right," said Lassiter. "We did it. All

these years Ben was holding that over our heads. Oh, he quit for a while, but when he started up again I knew I had to kill him. Just like I have to kill you."

Hardy backed up as Lassiter advanced. All he could think of was that his sweat was making the cuts on his face hurt. Lassiter knocked the photos out of Hardy's hands. Hardy cringed. Lassiter sneered and spit at Hardy. Hardy picked up his hand to wipe his face. Lassiter slapped it down.

Click. For some reason his reflexes had been a little slow, but now they were functioning. Hardy's mind cowered in a gray mental corner and the reflexes that the army had programmed for just such an occasion went into action.

He caught Lassiter's offending hand and bent it back. Surprised, Lassiter tried to shake him off and put his free left hand around Hardy's throat. Hardy grabbed at Lassiter's left forearm and squeezed, trying to get Lassiter to relax the pressure on his throat. It was no use. Lassiter was too strong.

Hardy released Lassiter's forearm and concentrated on the other hand. The pressure grew worse . . . in a few seconds he would be out. Hardy used all he had in bending Lassiter's right hand back. Snap. Lassiter's wrist was broken.

Lassiter screamed and let go of Hardy's neck. Hardy hammered at Lassiter's nose, breaking it and sending Lassiter to the floor. Hardy kicked in one rib and was trying for the rest of them when the New York Police, led by Detective Gerald Friday and Lieutenant Luis Mendoza of the Mexican Federal Police, broke in the door.

Chapter Fourteen

Hardy was back in his apartment . . . Melanie had fed Holmes and was waiting for him. She poured him a glass of champagne and while he sipped and relaxed and tried to forget about Lassiter, she whipped up a cheese souffle.

The champagne washed away the sour taste that came when he had gotten sick after the police had pulled him away from Lassiter.

Melanie put the food in front of him. "There, eat . . . and tell me."

He ate and told her . . . all about how Ben had left the clue in the crossword puzzle book and how Ben had been blackmailing Lassiter and Ricci and Leon all these years for raping and murdering a girl back in college and how Lassiter had killed Ben in Mexico and how Mendoza thought that Lassiter and Hardy were Ben's partners in a drug smuggling operation and had had tails on both of them and how Hardy had ditched Mendoza in his Buick thinking it was Lassiter and . . .

Melanie listened and watched as Hardy ate the souffle. She poured more champagne and lit two cigarettes. "Gerald Friday called me today."

Hardy took a long satisfied drag of his cigarette. "Really, what did he want?"

"To see me. Go out with me. That sort of thing."

"And? . . ."

She smiled. "And what?"

"Are you going to see him?"

"I don't know . . . that remains to be seen. But I'm here now . . . Tony."

Hardy remembered the use of his middle name with pleasure. Her intent couldn't have been clearer.

The phone rang. Those reflexes which had been so helpful earlier did the worse thing they could have. Even though his mind was else where, his reflexes told his hand to answer the phone. He did.

"Hi stud, it's me, Ruby. My plane just landed. I'm sorry I didn't call. I wanted to surprise you. Pat, I'm so horny for you I'm shaking. I'll be right over." And she hung up the phone before he could say a word.

Hardy looked at Melanie and then at the phone and then back at Melanie.

"What's wrong, Tony?" She touched his face ever so lightly with her long tapered fingers, sending a chill through his aroused and troubled being. Images of the light caramel that were her breasts pervaded.

"What's wrong?" she repeated, "More problems?"

"Problems?" he thought frantically. "She didn't know the half of it."

Visit us at <u>www.speakingvolumes.us</u>

Visit us at www.speakingvolumes.us

A PATRICK HARDY MYSTERY

SPY AND DIE

martin meyers

Published by SpeakingVolumes

Visit us at www.speakingvolumes.us

Visit us at www.speakingvolumes.us

**FIND OUT WHY
THE CRITICS LOVE THE
HISTORICAL MYSTERIES OF
MAAN MEYERS**

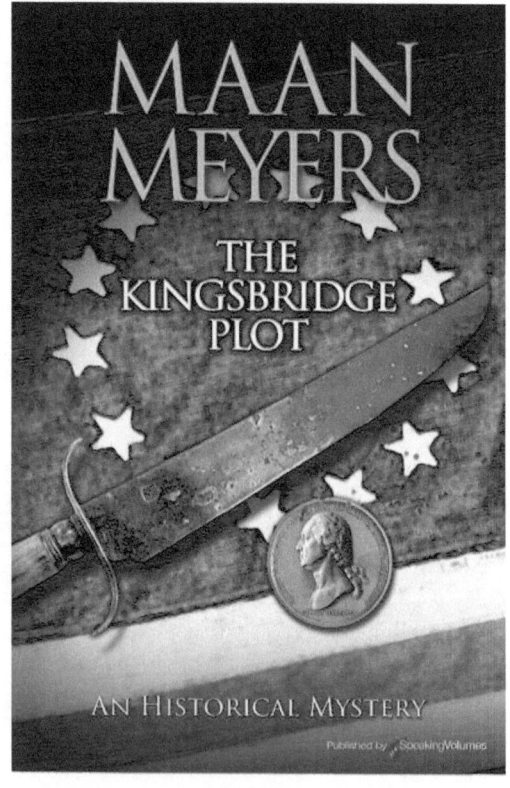

Visit us at www.speakingvolumes.us